RELIEF PITCHER

by DICK FRIENDLICH

Cover by Mort Künstler

SCHOLASTIC BOOK SERVICES

Published by Scholastic Book Services, a division
of Scholastic Magazines, Inc., New York, N. Y.

Copyright © 1964 by Dick Friendlich. This Scholastic Book
Services edition is published by arrangement with
The Westminster Press.

1st printing.................... February 1966

Printed in the U.S.A.

CHAPTER 1

THE HUSKY RIGHT-HANDER took his last warm-up pitch from the box, the catcher shot the ball down to second base, and the infielders fired it once around the diamond before the plate signaled that it was time to resume play.

The last man to catch the ball was the third baseman. He walked slowly toward the pitcher, his glove hanging by its strap from his left wrist as he rubbed the ball vigorously between the palms of his hands.

In his loose-fitting gray uniform, the third baseman looked neither slim nor stocky, but somewhere in between. In height, he was neither tall nor short, perhaps two or three inches under six feet. He walked with the relaxed, slouching gait of the trained athlete.

Below the peaked bill of the baseball cap covering his dark hair — a shade off coal black — the third baseman's eyes were a mild blue, his features sharp-planed. His name was Peter Bedford Conroy, and at the moment he was not only the third baseman but the manager of the Winston Wildcats in the Class C Central Plains League.

1

"O.K., Robbie, only three to go," he said cheerfully as he deposited the ball in the outstretched glove of the pitcher, a heavily muscled 19-year-old with a harassed look on his round face.

"Yeah, only three," Glenn Robertson said, and wiped the perspiration from his forehead with his sleeve.

"Don't give Woodman anything inside," Conroy advised, and trotted back to third base, dark brows almost meeting in a look of concern. He wished Robbie had sounded a bit more confident about facing the three Vernon City hitters coming up in the bottom of the ninth inning.

Pete glanced over his shoulder at the wooden scoreboard above the brown board fence, both badly in need of a paint job.

| VISITORS | 021 | 230 | 011 |
| VERNON CITY | 140 | 120 | 00 |

Robertson, a fidgety, jerky workman on the mound, had pitched well enough since relieving Dave Elias with two men on base in the sixth. That was more than could be said of the sore-armed Elias in relief of Luke Bosler, who had started. Well, Pete thought, the Cats were still on top, 10–8. He looked around to check the position of the Wildcat outfielders, then cast his eyes quickly upward to the flagpole above the rickety grandstand to judge the direction of the wind.

It was purely a reflex action on Conroy's part, for the flag hung down limply, as it had all night.

2

There was not a breath of movement in the air. Around the arc lights that illuminated the field, swarms of insects swirled and darted.

Those lights, Conroy thought in disgust. It's a wonder someone doesn't get skulled by a fly ball every game.

Once a ball got above the lights, he had discovered, it virtually disappeared from the fielder's straining sight, and he had to look for it all over again when it started falling back past them.

And the insects! Every now and then, a few would make a foray down from the lights to sting some unsuspecting shirt-sleeved fan in the stands.

"Summer's going to be early this year," the natives said knowingly around the cities of the Central Plains League. "You can always tell by the warm spring."

Pete wondered what summer was going to be like, if this was only spring. It was May, and Vernon City was no ski resort, that was certain.

As he had more than once before, Pete Conroy wondered just what he was doing here, only a short period in time but a million miles away, figuratively speaking, from Hornet Stadium, with its curving double-decked stands and its seating capacity for more than 40,000 spectators.

He brought his thoughts back to the problem of the moment as Woodman stepped into the batter's box. The powerful youngster hit right-handed and swung from the heels — strictly a pull hitter. But he was not fast, and Conroy played him deep on the dirt part of the diamond and close to the foul line, confident Woodman would not bunt.

Robertson pitched, a fast ball waist high and inside. Woodman brought his bat around with a whipping motion and the ball came down the third-base line as a gray blur.

Pete instinctively lunged to his right, stretching his gloved left hand across his body. It was simply a "stab and grab" attempt; on a ball that was hit that swiftly, an infielder could do little more than reach and hope it bounced right.

This one did. It struck in the dirt, two feet beyond the bag at third base and just inside the line, and came up sharply into Conroy's glove. Pete straightened, saw in that instant that he had time to set himself as Woodman lumbered down the first-base path, then gunned the ball like a projectile on the long cross-diamond throw. It beat the runner by three steps.

As he walked toward the mound, the thought flashed through Pete's mind that Joe Troyer, the Hornets' third baseman, couldn't have handled that smash any better, if he could have handled it at all. Unfortunately —

He buried the speculation about Troyer under his irritation with Robertson.

"You threw that right in his wheelhouse," he said accusingly. "You trying to get somebody killed?"

Robertson pawed at the rubber with his toeplate.

4

"Sorry, Skipper," he muttered. "It got away from me."

"O.K., but bear down, kid. Only two to go."

Conroy went back to third base. He had not yet become accustomed to being addressed as "Skipper" by players near his own age, which was 24, or only a few years younger, like Robertson. He had been a manager for almost two months, since the day the Hornets, not without regret, had decided he was no longer useful to them — through no fault of his own.

Robertson, sweating freely, walked the batter after going to three-and-two on him. Conroy immediately trotted over to talk to him, and Gus Liebman, the Cats' catcher, joined them. The pitcher groused at the umpire's call of ball four, but Pete told him to forget it.

"Keep it low to this guy and we'll get two," he said encouragingly.

Robertson kept it low, beyond doubt. His first two deliveries were in the dirt and Liebman did well to block both and hold the runner at first.

The catcher was a rangy youngster, in his first season of professional baseball, signed out of college. He was quick, with a good arm. If he could learn to hit a curve, Conroy had decided, Liebman would be a big leaguer and a good one.

After Robbie's second pitch had skidded into Liebman's mitt, Conroy wheeled and made a throwing motion. Down in the bullpen, which was placed in front of the left-field seats, a lanky southpaw named Kit Randall stood up and began to throw leisurely to Harry Hall, the number two catcher.

Randall had warmed up intermittently since Robertson had come on in the sixth, and Conroy knew he should be ready without much more work in the pen. If only Robbie could hold on, he thought gloomily. Randall might come on and strike out everybody, but he was also just as likely to miss the plate by three feet. Like most young pitchers in the low minors, the southpaw had quite a bit of stuff, but also quite a bit of trouble putting the ball where he wanted it.

Come on, Robbie, get it over, Pete pleaded silently. Robertson threw three straight balls, and the Vernon fans began to clap rhythmically. Conroy groaned to himself as the pitcher didn't even get the oh-and-three pitch, the "automatic strike," near the plate.

Once again Pete asked for time and went to the mound, an action that drew jeers from the stands and brought the plate umpire, Steadman, out to join him with an impatient attitude.

"Come on, Conroy," he said testily. "Either let this man pitch or bring in your new one. It's getting late."

"Sure thing, Sam," Pete said with an ingratiating smile, and beckoned toward the bullpen. He saw no point in ruffling the umpire unnecessarily.

Randall took the ball from the disconsolate Robertson and took his eight allotted warm-up throws.

Deke Holleran yelled at Conroy from the dugout. "You want Clem down there?" he asked, pointing to the dugout. Pete hesitated, then shook his head. He would stand or fall with Randall. The Wildcats went home to Winston for a game next day and two more the following day, and Pete wanted Clem Bassett fresh for tomorrow, with Larry Kavic for one game of the doubleheader and Bosler, he supposed, for the second one. Bosler had worked only one inning tonight and should be able to come back two days later.

In fact, he would have to, Conroy told himself grimly. With Johnny Hale's arm so sore he couldn't comb his hair, the Wildcats were a little short on pitchers.

If you could call some of 'em pitchers, Pete growled to himself. The Hornets, who had a working agreement with Winston to provide players, hadn't sent the Cats any budding Don Drysdales.

To the delight of the crowd and Pete's increasing mental distress, Randall walked the bases full. Mindful of Steadman's impatience, Conroy trotted only halfway to the hill, yelled, "Just get the ball over the plate, Kit, that's all," and went back again.

Even I could do that, he fumed inwardly. Who knows, maybe someone might catch the blasted ball.

Randall improved somewhat, going to three-and-two before he put the next delivery so high that Liebman had to jump to stop it. The runner from

7

third jogged home, leaving the bases full and the home team only one run behind with one out.

It was more than Pete Conroy could stand. His face was taut with frustration as he barked, "Time, Sam," to the umpire. Then he turned toward the dugout and called to Deke Holleran.

"Grab a glove and get out here, Deke. You play third."

The infielder looked astonished. He could play third base, but so far as he could tell, the Cats already had someone in that position.

Conroy strode toward the mound, where Randall waited with a forlorn expression. "All right, Kit, it's one of those nights. You'll have it next time."

The plate umpire came up on Liebman's heels. "Now look, Conroy," he rasped, "you're not going to hold a summit meeting after every pitch. Get back where you belong and let's try to play a little baseball!"

Pete's blue eyes twinkled. For the moment, he was enjoying himself. "I've got a right to ask for time when I change pitchers, haven't I?" he asked in an aggrieved tone.

Steadman glanced out toward the empty bullpen. "Sure you have," he said loudly. "Bring on your new one."

"I don't have to bring him on. He's here. Me."

The umpire stared as though he had not heard correctly. Liebman and Randall looked startled. Then Steadman recovered his dignity.

"You're pitching?" he inquired with exaggerated

politeness. "All right, you've got eight coming. Let's get going."

"I didn't know you could pitch, Skipper," Liebman said in wonderment. "What are you going to throw?"

The glow of triumph that had followed the brief confounding of the umpire evaporated, leaving Pete feeling like a man about to make his first dive in a submarine. But he was not going to display any lack of self-confidence in front of his catcher.

"I've fooled around some with pitching," he said gruffly, which was not exactly true, nor entirely false. He *had* pitched batting practice a few times in the minors, but this was not the ideal situation in which to inform Liebman that this was his first appearance on the mound during a game.

"I'm not going to monkey with any trick stuff, Gus," he told the catcher. "The fast ball only, high and tight, then low and away. I want 'em to hit it. Just give me the target, understand?"

Liebman nodded. "Right, Skip. Let 'er rip."

Conroy toed the mound. With the bases full, he could pitch from a full windup. He tried his first warm-up delivery as a sweeping side-arm, thrown with all the power he could muster. It struck Liebman's mitt with a satisfying noise, and the catcher nodded approvingly as he returned the ball.

The other Wildcat infielders gathered behind Pete as he continued his warm-up, gripped by curiosity.

"Take a good look, Chuck," Pete said out of the corner of his mouth to Hostett, the first baseman. "It may be your last one at this pitcher."

Hostett's uncertain laugh was echoed by Halligan, the fuzz-cheeked second baseman.

"All right, play ball!" Steadman yelped, and Liebman came out for one last word.

"You can really burn 'em in, Skipper," he said respectfully. "These guys may not even see it."

Pete took a deep breath, an unnecessary pull at the peak of his cap, and bent over to grasp the resin bag. For an instant, he regretted the angry impatience that had brought him out here. He could end by looking several kinds of fool. But he wanted to put a finish to this long, drawn-out night. Whether the Cats won or lost this game didn't seem important anymore.

He considered the batter, a right-handed swinger named Gibson who had two hits and a walk so far, but who had also struck out twice.

Conroy peered in at Liebman's sign — fast one on the letters. Pete rocked forward, arms loose, rocked back with a wide, swinging motion of his left leg, and cut loose.

The ball appeared to Gibson to be coming at him from the vicinity of third base and he fell back hastily. It was not even close to him, however, and Steadman called it a strike.

Pete stifled a chuckle. He thought the umpire might have given him the edge on that call. Throwing sidearm came naturally to an infielder who had to make a quick peg, although when he

10

had time to set himself for it, Pete threw overhand.

But the sidearm cross fire could be intimidating to an inexperienced batter, and Gibson fitted that frame. Pete checked the runner at third and pitched again, as Liebman came up from his crouch and set his mitt low and outside. Gibson was ready to back away again, but saw the ball would be somewhere near the strike zone. He swung tentatively and too late.

" 'Atsa way to burn 'em in, Skip!" Halligan hollered behind Pete. Liebman signaled for the same pitch and Pete made a brushing movement with his glove against his uniform. The catcher called for low and inside, and again Pete gave the brushoff sign, not without amusement.

Just as though I had two different pitches, he thought. With a two-strike, no-ball count, he preferred to waste one high, hoping the hitter would swing at the bad ball. Liebman, by a process of elimination, arrived at that signal.

Using the same sweeping motion and wide leg kick, Pete fired, over the plate but at eye level. Gibson couldn't have hit it with a snowshoe, but he swung anyway, and went away from the plate kicking at his bat.

Hey, I struck out a man, Pete thought in pleased surprise. Not that Gibson was any Roger Maris as a hitter.

"Here's the last one," Holleran chirped. "The bus is waiting, fellows."

The Vernon City manager sent up a pinch hit-

11

ter, a left-handed swinger Pete had never seen before. He decided he would try to jam him on the fists with his first delivery. Maybe the fellow was a fall-away pull hitter who would lift it over the right-field fence. But Pete was certain of one thing in his mind — he wasn't going to try to hit corners and maybe walk the batter. Anything but that.

He pitched. The ball was a little more inside than he had wanted it. The batter stepped back slightly and chopped at it. He hit it, not with the "good wood," as the players called the solid part of the bat, but just above his hands. It slithered on the ground directly at Halligan, the second baseman.

Easy chance, Pete thought expectantly. It was all over.

Halligan waited, feet apart, braced to make the throw as soon as he picked up the ball. It slipped beneath his hands and through his legs into right center field, and as the fans yelled exultantly, the tying and winning runs scored.

Halligan stood with his back to the infield, looking toward the spot where the ball had bounded, as though he were afraid to turn and face the manager.

Conroy sighed and stuffed his glove into his hip pocket. His shoulders drooped slightly at the disappointing finish. A smarter, more experienced fielder would have charged in instead of waiting for the ball, playing it rather than letting the ball play him. Or if he had waited, he would have kneeled to block it should he fail to field it cleanly.

But Halligan, less than a year off a high school diamond, had neglected to "drop the apron," as the saying went. Conroy would remind him of it once more, but not right now. The kid probably felt worse about the error than he, the manager, did, which was bad enough.

Liebman, a dejected expression on his boyish features, fell in stride with Conroy as they walked with the other Wildcats to the clubhouse.

"Tough break, Skipper," he said sympathetically. "That pitch should have got 'em out. It was a good slider and the guy was lucky to get a piece of it."

Pete glanced up quickly at his tall backstop. "What do you mean, slider?"

Liebman seemed puzzled by the question.

"Well, it looked like a slider. Anyway, it broke down and in on him. It wasn't just the hummer, like the ones you threw to Gibson."

Conroy blinked.

"Is that right?" He sounded indifferent. But he was pleased in rather a vague way. An old joke came to his mind — about the man who was asked if he could play the piano and who replied that he did not know because he had never tried.

"I must be getting loopy," he murmured to himself, and followed Liebman into the musty little locker room.

CHAPTER 2

WHENEVER PETE CONROY had difficulty getting to sleep, eventually his mind would settle upon Dixie Fleming, The Actor.

This was one of those nights.

The Wildcats had boarded their chartered bus and driven the 70 miles back to Winston immediately after the game. It was nearly two o'clock before Pete got to bed in his small apartment, and he seemed too tired to sleep at once. Frustration over the defeat, over the Cats' erratic pitching staff, over the entire unfortunate chain of events that had brought him to a job for which, he was beginning to believe, he was wholly unfitted, churned through his mind.

He turned over and punched the pillow. Dixie Fleming, the gift of Mercer Falls to baseball. Dixie Fleming, now a mere 21, with the world by the tail on a downhill pull. And, Pete reflected bitterly, a natural-born ballplayer, sure to become one of the game's big stars.

Barring accident, of course, he thought sardonically. Accident of the kind that had swept away

Pete Conroy's hard apprenticeship in the minor leagues, and with it his future in the majors.

Conroy had never envied Fleming's native ability, so superior to his own. Pete could do no one thing superlatively, but he could do several things fairly well, or he would never have reached the Hornets at all. He was the jack-of-all-positions, the utility fielder.

He had applied himself intensely to the task of assimilating the demands of each spot on the field, and enjoyed one satisfactory full season with the Hornets before Dixie Fleming appeared.

At various times in his brief career, Pete had played at every position except first base and catcher — and, until last night, pitcher.

He had good hands, he could run, and he had an exceptional arm. He could whip the ball across the infield from third or deep short with a quick snap, or from the outfield shadows to the plate on one bounce.

Certainly, he was not a great infielder, or even a very good outfielder, but he was better than average as either. Had he concentrated at one position, Pete believed, he could have been a regular, even though he had never been a menace to league batting records. He was essentially a place hitter who didn't deliver the long ball. But in his one complete season with the Hornets, he had hit .258, quite acceptable for a player who did not have the advantage of facing a pitcher every day.

In all, a most satisfying year for Pete. He appeared in more than half the Hornets' games, sometimes only an inning or two for defensive purposes, sometimes as a pinch hitter against left-handers, occasionally a full game to rest some veteran's aching legs or replace an ailing regular.

Then along came Dixie Fleming, and Pete Conroy was now riding shotgun on a herd of kids in a rinky-dink town in the midst of Nowhere, U.S.A.

Fleming came up to the Hornets from Indianapolis, a big, raw-boned youngster with curly blond hair and pink-cheeked good looks. The Hornets had paid $75,000 for his signature on a contract two years before and it appeared as though they might have made a good bargain. He had hit .348 for Indy and led the league in putouts and assists for outfielders.

Dan Ricketts, the Hornets' president, and Joe Metz, the head of their farm club organization, thought Fleming might be just the boy to get the team out of the second division, where it had been resting for several seasons.

Fleming knew he was good. He did not brag offensively, but he exuded confidence and showed none of the deference to the Hornet veterans that might be expected from a 20-year-old rookie. He wasn't disrespectful toward them, but he wasn't exactly respectful either.

Pete Conroy had been more amused than irritated by Dixie's brash bounciness. The Hornet outfielders, particularly Hardy Clampett, the center fielder of the preceding season, found Fleming less amusing, for a number of reasons. None of them made any impression on the manager, Fred Kearns.

He issued a veiled warning early in spring training.

"I don't want anybody trying to put the spurs to this kid. He'll quiet down when he learns his way around."

The manager might have saved his breath. The rookie was oblivious not only to the sarcastic digs directed at him when Kearns was out of earshot but to the frontal challenges as well. In the meantime, he hit .450 in the first dozen exhibition games and roamed the outfield as though it were his responsibility alone.

It was soon evident that Fleming never doubted that he could hit any pitcher, outrun any throw, or catch any ball to which he could get close enough to wave at. Apparently it did not occur to him that it might be easier for the left fielder, for example, to move 10 feet to his left to make a catch than it would be for him, Fleming, to run 40 feet to his right to accomplish the same purpose.

This led to a few near collisions. Willie Gaines, the Hornets' right fielder, once growled at Fleming that he would cut him off at the knees if the rookie ever ran in front of him again. Willie felt he did not need help on fly balls hit right to him.

"I'm sorry, Willie," Fleming said brightly, treating Gaines as an equal. "Down at Indianapolis, I got so used to hearing the other fielders yell, 'All yours, Dixie,' that I just go after hits like that one automatically."

Gaines, in his eighth season in the majors, was too astounded to say anything.

Dixie got his nickname during an exhibition game against Detroit.

Pitcher Jim Bunning, facing Fleming in the first inning, brushed him back with a fast ball under the chin. Another batter might have leaned back from the waist, but Dixie dropped as though shot, losing his bat and protective helmet in the process. He arose with a dismayed look in Bunning's direction, and took his time putting himself together, brushing off his uniform, and running a hand through his blond hair.

Wexler, the Hornets' first baseman, said loudly, "Man, he bailed out fast on that one, didn't he?"

Before anyone in the dugout could add comment, Bunning served a low curve outside, and Dixie, timing it perfectly, whacked a line drive into right center field.

It was a good two-base hit, but the right fielder moved quickly to cut off the ball. Corky Schmidt, coaching at third, held up both hands as Fleming turned second base.

If the rookie saw the sign to stop there, he ignored it, for he did not hesitate to come on toward third. The relay from the second baseman reached third simultaneously with Dixie, but he evaded the tag with a beautiful hook slide.

From the bench, Pete Conroy could see the startled look on Fleming's face after he got up and heard what Schmidt had to say. Pete grinned. The Dutchman was old enough to be Dixie's father, and he did not like rookies running through his signs, even in exhibition games.

A long sacrifice fly brought Fleming home. As he reached the dugout, Fred Kearns said mildly, "The pitch that decked you didn't look that close."

"It wasn't," the rookie said with a flashing smile. "I figured he was setting me up for low and away and maybe if I acted a little gun-shy, he'd put it where I could hit it to right field. He did, too."

Kearns, burly as a bear, gave him a searching look, not quite sure whether he was being kidded. But sincerity was written all over Fleming's face and the manager merely grunted.

Wexler could not contain himself. "Great Smoky!" he exploded. "Now we got an actor."

And so Dixie Fleming became The Actor.

In all justice, Pete had to admit that the rookie did not seem to play consciously to the grandstand. And as he continued to hit over .300 and field his position in fancy fashion once the regular season had begun, the Hornets continued to call him The Actor, but usually without malice.

Occasionally Fleming's antics aroused anger in a veteran. Gaines was ready to take him on after another near collision in right field. Corky Schmidt talked the furious outfielder out of the idea of physical combat.

"It was my ball all the way," Willie stormed. "I don't aim to get killed by some bush-league showboat. I'll kill him first."

"Showboat maybe, but he ain't no busher, Willie," the coach said soothingly. "You want him to

19

dog it instead? We're in third place and the kid has helped put us there. Personally I wouldn't object to a slice of that World Series dough."

The Hornets didn't make the World Series, eventually finishing fourth, their highest ranking in several seasons. By the middle of June, however, they were still third. Pete Conroy was hitting .249 and playing part of the time in half the games, usually at third base or shortstop. Now and then, however, he was sent to left field in the late innings when the Hornets wanted to protect a lead. Gus Sondheim, the regular, hit the long ball, but he was no defensive standout.

Pete was in left field when it happened — June 18, a date he was not likely to forget. The Hornets led the Gold Sox, 4–1 and Kearns sent him to left field as the Sox came up for the top of the ninth.

There were two out and a man on second when the pinch hitter, Pritchard, stepped up to the plate. He was a left-handed pull hitter who could lift the ball out of the park. The Hornet outfield shifted around toward right field for him, with Gaines near the line, Fleming in right center, and Pete in left center.

Pritchard swung late on a slider and raised a looping little fly behind second base. Pete came in on it quickly as Tex White, the shortstop, raced out on the grass.

Pete had judged the ball accurately and knew he could make the catch without difficulty. He made a quick moving motion with his right hand to signify that he had it. Chuck Mackey, the second baseman, had also started after the ball, but saw he could not reach it. "Conroy's!" he shouted.

That was to warn White, who had his eye on the descending ball and not on Pete, to leave it to the left fielder. White stopped at once and the ball dropped into Pete's glove at the same time that Dixie Fleming, coming like the wind from right center, swerved at the last possible moment to avoid running into him.

He did not quite make it. His left shoulder struck Pete a glancing blow and as he crossed behind Conroy, he stepped on the latter's exposed right heel with his spikes.

Both men went down. Pete held on to the ball, his first reaction blind anger at whoever had run into him. Then he saw the blood welling up over the back of his shoe through the shredded stocking, and he began to hurt.

He preferred not to think about that any more.

Pete remembered with some bitterness that the doctors had emphasized how lucky he was. Another half inch, they said, and the spikes might have severed the main tendon. Instead, there would be no permanent damage from the spike wounds, deep though they might be.

They were equally confident that no permanent damage would result from the removal of the torn cartilage in his right knee, twisted under him as he fell.

"It's a routine operation these days," the doctors said cheerfully, "No more difficult than taking out your tonsils. In a couple of months, you'll be as good as new."

From the medical viewpoint, they were proved absolutely correct. From the baseball viewpoint, they were not.

Dixie Fleming was among those who visited him in the hospital, but only once. The rookie obviously felt terrible about the accident. He seemed so miserable, so genuinely distressed, that Pete refrained from saying what he wanted to, which was that Fleming had no business in his territory. Besides, his knee pained him and he was too depressed to start any altercation.

At least, Pete was in that frame of mind until Dixie, rising to leave, said somewhat defensively, "You know, Pete, it really was my ball as much as yours."

The audacity of that statement not only astounded Conroy but infuriated him.

"Clean out your ears, showboat," he said hoarsely. "Mackey yelled it was mine loud enough for everyone to hear. If you hadn't been so busy grandstanding all over the park, you would have been behind me, where you belonged."

Dixie got very red in the face. "All right, if that's the way you feel about it," he said stiffly and left.

The Hornet players, Kearns, and even the president, Ricketts, were all faithful visitors to Pete during his three weeks in the hospital. They brought him more books than he could read in a year and enough fruit to stock an orchard. The only thing Pete resented was a remark attributed to Kearns that he read in the sports pages.

"Losing Conroy is a tough break," the manager told writers. "He's a valuable man. But it would have been tougher if Fleming had been the man who was hurt."

It was true enough, Pete had to concede, but he wished Kearns hadn't said it out loud. From the Hornets' standpoint, a utility man was expendable, but Dixie Fleming certainly was not.

The Hornets sent Pete home to San Francisco, his leg in a cast, and in the two months of inactivity that followed, Pete developed a rather philosophical attitude about the injury, and about Dixie Fleming too.

The rookie hadn't tried to hurt him, Pete reflected. Dixie was like a big playful hound who chased everything in sight, and probably would never change. Pete could not generate any deep-rooted feeling of a wrong that had to be avenged, although he knew he could never be counted among Fleming's admirers.

At least he felt that way until he rejoined the Hornets on September 1.

The players had welcomed him warmly and joshed him about getting fat while loafing. Actually, he had lost weight. Dixie Fleming said, "Hi, Conroy, glad you're back," in an offhand manner that gave no indication he even remembered having anything to do with Pete's absence.

Except for the two scars, which would fade with time, there was no outward evidence that

Pete had ever been injured. There was no pain in his leg, nor any stiffness.

But it was not the same as before. He was slower than he had been — a step, a fraction of a second, no more. Some of the edge had been lost in the reflex action of his leg and it made the difference between reaching a ground ball and feeling it flick the fingers of the glove; the difference between beating the catcher's throw to second on a steal and being tagged out.

And eventually it made the difference between a major leaguer and a minor leaguer.

Pete realized this within a week after he came back, and Fred Kearns sensed it before the season had ended.

Pete spent the first days chasing grounders and fungoes, and was at batting practice early and late to regain the co-ordination he might have lost through misuse.

His first chance to play came in a game with the Eagles. The Hornets trailed, 2–1, going into the last of the eighth, and when Gus Sondheim drew a walk to open it, Kearns sent Pete in to run for him.

Corky Schmidt flashed the bunt sign, even though the Eagles' third baseman was in on the grass, anticipating it, and their first baseman was ready to charge as soon as the pitcher delivered. Joe Troyer, the batter, was an accomplished bunter, and with a reasonably fast runner at first, the maneuver ought to advance the man even though the opposition was ready for it.

24

Pete got what he thought was a good jump on the pitcher's move, and Troyer dumped one slowly down the third-base line. The third baseman made a fine pickup, took one quick look toward Conroy going down the line, and threw to second just in time to get him on the force play.

There was surprise and chagrin on the Hornet bench, because the play had been perfectly executed. Pete himself was disappointed, but could only assume that Troyer's bunt had been hit harder than he thought.

The feeling of doubt, however, did not begin until two days later. Filling in at shortstop for Tex White, Pete failed to reach a ball he thought he had. It was a sharp grounder in the hole between short and third and skipped under his reaching hand. He had made the same play innumerable times before.

Again, he did not quite get to a fly ball in left field, though he had it in his sights all the way. He had to try for a diving catch and missed. Something akin to fear gnawed at him. He had not misjudged the ball; he was certain when he started for it that he would get under it. Yet he had not.

"Your knee bothering you, Pete?" Fred Kearns asked him. Pete answered truthfully that it did not; it felt as strong as it ever had. But he knew why Kearns had asked.

The manager did not refer to the injury again, but he did not use Pete in any close games again in the last two weeks of the season.

Then, on the last day, when it was all over, Kearns said, "What do you plan to do this winter, Pete? Same as last year, selling bulldozers?"

Pete grinned. "Selling bulldozers" was the manager's description of his off-season employment with a firm of construction engineers. Pete's duties were confined to the office and he went twice a week to night school for courses in business management. That would be his future when his baseball days were over, but right now he was not much more than a clerk. He told Kearns his plans were the same as they had been the year before.

"That give you any time for exercise? Can you get out and run occasionally?"

"I always do. There's a park near where I live. I go there weekends."

"Fine. Like to see you in good shape in Florida."

Pete understood.

I'll be all right in the spring, he told himself doggedly. I'll run a lot.

And he did. When he reported to the Hornets' spring training site on March 1, he had never felt in better condition. Within a week, Pete knew that the little extra bit of speed had not come back. Infield hits he did not beat out, grounders he could not reach, bore out what he feared.

Fred Kearns realized it too, and it saddened him. He liked Pete Conroy because he was not a troublemaker, he hustled on every play, and before his injury, had performed to the limit of his ability.

But the revitalized Hornets were setting their sights high this season. The front office believed that the pennant was not out of the question. Kearns knew the team could not afford a light-hitting utility man whose defensive value — his principal asset to the club — had been reduced, no matter what the reason. It was a tough break for Pete Conroy, but he might cost the team half a dozen games a swifter man could save.

The manager discussed it at length with President Ricketts and Joe Metz. The farm system head thought Conroy should go to Austin, a Class A team.

"He can get by in that league," Metz offered. "He'd probably help the club a lot. Who knows, he may get back that extra step, playing every day."

Ricketts snapped his fingers as an idea came to him. "What about him for Winston?" he said. "As a playing manager? Might be just the ticket for the club."

Metz was astounded. Kearns was surprised, but he stayed out of the argument that followed. It was not his province to decide where players should be sent.

Metz contended that Conroy lacked the experience to manage a team made up principally of players in their first or second season of organized ball.

Ricketts waved aside that objection. "A manager doesn't have to be a hundred years old, Joe. Conroy's smart, he knows how the plays should be made and he can make them himself, probably better than anyone on the roster. Besides, he'll be getting his orders from here, and Grabhorn and Palmer will be out there from time to time."

Grabhorn and Palmer were the Hornets' chief scouts, who operated out of the hometown headquarters. Eventually, Metz had to agree to the move. He had no alternative once the president had made up his mind.

Pete Conroy had never admitted to himself that he was no longer useful to the Hornets, but he was not entirely unprepared for the information that he was being sent to the minor leagues. But, like Joe Metz, he was astounded to learn where he was being sent.

"Class C?" he demanded incredulously. "As a manager? I've never managed even a sandlot team."

"I know it," Metz said gruffly, and Pete had the distinct impression that Joe did not approve. "But the owners of the Winston club would like a playing manager, especially one just out of the big leagues. It's not one of the clubs we own outright; we've got only a working agreement with them and we supply 'em with players we want to develop.

"Besides, with an 18-man roster, a fellow like yourself who can fill in anyplace is especially valuable. We'll try to put a representative team there; naturally we want to win the pennant if we can. But we're also interested in the progress of our young ballplayers. That's where you can help."

Pete did not know whether to be grateful or resentful about the Hornets' decision. The fact that he could not, at this stage of his training, make half as much money with the construction company as he would remaining in the Hornet organization was one factor in his decision.

The other was the idea that he might, in some unexplained manner, regain the split-second extra step if he could play regularly. It was more of a hope than a conviction, but he could not abandon it.

So it was that he came to be turning restlessly on a hot night in the city of Winston, reflecting on the tricks of fate, and above all, on The Actor.

CHAPTER 3

PETE CONROY rapped a grounder to Halligan, who scooped it up gracefully just as the buzzer sounded to signify that it was now the turn of the visiting Bellview Bells to take fielding practice.

"Why couldn't he have done that last night?" Pete grumbled as he went to the Winston dugout. The Cats trooped in after him to slouch on the bench, and down the right-field line, Winston's starting pitcher, Clem Bassett, began to throw leisurely to Harry Hall.

Tommy Clauson, sports editor of the Winston *Register*, was standing by the water cooler waiting for Conroy. He was a round-faced young man, volubly enthusiastic about the game, and Pete found him quite likable.

"Who's going tomorrow, Number One?"

Clauson usually addressed Pete that way because that was the numeral on his uniform and his question was routine — the pitchers for the next day.

"Whitey Ford in the opener and Jack Sanford in the second one," Pete said, not smiling. "That's all I've got left."

Clauson chortled. "Aw, come on, Pete. Is it Kavic and Bosler?"

"You ought to be managing this club instead of me," Pete said, grinning. "Kavic and Bosler it is, providing I don't have to use either of 'em tonight."

The sportswriter seemed pleased at his own perception. "Hey, what about last night? The box score shows you pitched to two batters last night. I didn't know you'd ever pitched."

"I still haven't. No one else could find the plate and I wanted to get back here before daylight."

"No, seriously," Clauson persisted. "Had you ever tried it before?"

"No, Tommy. I've pitched batting practice a few times, that's all. Never in a game."

"Can you put any stuff on the ball?" Clauson asked earnestly, and Pete laughed.

"Oh, sure, everyone can. The problem is getting it over in a regular game."

"I don't know whether you're kidding me or not," the sportswriter said plaintively.

"No, I mean that," Pete said, surprised that Clauson was not aware of the practice. "Did you ever watch a bunch of players warm up by playing catch? They all try to make the ball do tricks — knucklers, screwballs, rainbow curves, all that junk. I've heard that Clete Boyer of the Yankees has a slider as good as anything you'd see. He'd probably have trouble controlling it, though, and besides, he's too good a third baseman."

31

"Did you throw any trick stuff last night?"

"Ask Gus," Pete said mischievously, gesturing toward Liebman, who had been listening with unconcealed interest. Then, before the catcher could say anything, Pete said, "I never did show you my fork ball, did I, Gus?"

"Do you have one?"

"Do I have one?" Conroy said in wounded tones. "Among the best. I didn't want to show 'em everything at once."

Laughter greeted this, and Conroy walked over to watch Bassett, a stumpy right-hander, warming up. Actually, he could throw a fork ball, a fluttering half-speed delivery, except that it might very well hit someone in the dugout as often as it got near the plate. The Hornets had a pitcher, Joe Michaels, who specialized in the pitch and he had shown Pete how he held it — between the index and middle fingers. Conroy had tried throwing it for his own amusement, nothing more.

Bassett broke off a sharp curve as Pete came up behind Hall.

"That was a beauty, Clem," Pete called. Then he remarked to the catcher, "If he can get that over tonight, they won't see him. He's quick."

"Sure, he's quick," Hall said over his shoulder. "So are 50 other guys I know. It took Sandy Koufax four years before he could control his fast curve, and this kid ain't no Koufax."

Pete took a quick hold on his temper. Hall, he had learned, had a sour outlook generally. Undoubtedly it was rooted in his eight years of

32

knocking around the minors, never higher than Class A, and by now fully aware that he was never going to reach the big circuits. He had caught for Winston last season, and Pete suspected that Hall would have liked the job of manager for his own.

So he replied mildly that he knew there weren't many like Koufax of the Dodgers and that he would be satisfied if Bassett just stayed near the plate.

Bassett did that for six innings, lost control in the late stages, but staggered the distance to win, 10–5. The Wildcats had hammered three Bellview pitchers for a big early lead.

Sloppy but good, Pete thought. He had to work more on Clem's tendency to pitch too fast when he was in a difficult spot. Otherwise, it had been a satisfying contest. Pete had hit a single and a double and handled six chances at third base. None of them had been tough ones, but his hands and his arm were as good as ever, he told himself defiantly.

Besides, the victory had boosted Winston into a third-place tie in the league and might bring out a good crowd for the next day's doubleheader.

It did, and the fans applauded in appreciation as Larry Kavic beat the Bells handily in the opener, 6–1. Only one incident marred the game and that was a minor one. Fuzzy Deraine, the Cats' shortstop, was struck on the forearm by a pitch in the eighth, and the trainer advised him to sit out the rest of the day, though it appeared to be only a bruise.

But Deraine was in obvious pain, so Conroy moved to shortstop and put Deke Holleran at third, where he had less territory to protect.

Pete played shortstop in the second game, though, as it turned out, it did not make much difference who was at that position. Everything Luke Bosler threw, the Bells hit.

From his observation point behind the pitcher, it looked to Pete as though the young right-hander had as much stuff as he had ever showed. But it was one of those days, and by the second inning it was obvious that it was not one of Bosler's days, for sure. The black-browed hurler was both pained and angry at the manner in which his best pitches were being slammed, but the Bells had a 5–1 lead after three and Pete reluctantly waved Luke to the showers.

Kit Randall came in and the Bells quickly made it 9–2 on a combination of his own wildness and a couple of errors, one of them a costly mistake by Halligan.

The second baseman failed to make the pivot adequately on what appeared to be a sure double-play ball hit to Holleran. The runner sliding into second trying to break up the double play impelled Halligan to hurry his throw. It went into the dirt, Hostett could not dig it out, and two runs scored.

Halligan looked woebegone and Pete kicked moodily at the bag. The kid had looked gun-shy of those sliding spikes, and if he was, then he had better find another position or even another profession. Pete would spend all the time necessary with Halligan to help him with the all-important pivot play, because the Hornets, Joe Metz in particular, thought Halligan was a comer. Pete was beginning to have his doubts about that.

In the meantime, a weedy southpaw named Pence was keeping Winston well in check as Bellview continued to make runs. Randall was lifted for a pinch hitter in the sixth and Dave Elias came on, with no more success than his predecessors.

By that time, the Bells led, 12–3, and the fans were beginning to leave the park. Exasperated, Pete was of a mind not to waste any more of his pitchers in the lost cause, but the sight of Elias selecting a bat to lead off the bottom of the Wildcat eighth made him change it. Elias was an automatic out, and even with a nine-run deficit to make up, a manager was obliged to try.

"Gary, get a bat and swing for Dave," he directed Pelter, the reserve outfielder. "Come on, Harry, let's throw a few. I'll pitch the ninth."

The catcher grinned slyly as he picked up his mitt. "You been studying up on this?" he asked. "Gonna start a new career?"

"Cut it out," Pete growled, annoyed. "I don't want to use Robertson in a game that's already down the drain."

That was exactly the way he felt, but as he began to throw to Hall, Pete speculated on the possibility of taking on lost-cause relief jobs more frequently in the future. It would take some pressure off his erratic sore-armed staff. Furthermore, he reflected, it would be an interesting experiment. He might even throw the fork ball today for kicks.

When the announcement of the new pitcher was made over the loudspeaker, there was a buzz of interest in the stands and a few laughs could be heard. As he walked to the mound where Gus Liebman waited, Pete had the uncomfortable feeling that the fans believed he was going there to provide some comedy.

"Hey, Pete, is this amateur night?" the Bellview third-base coach called through cupped hands. Liebman smiled faintly.

"I'm not here to clown around, Gus," Pete said curtly. "Just give me the target. If I get ahead of a hitter, I might try a change-up — a fork ball."

"O.K., Skipper," Liebman said respectfully.

The Bellview lead-off batter in the inning watched with interest as Pete warmed up with the sidearm motion. Apparently, it made him cautious, for he was backing away from the first pitch which was far outside.

This guy isn't going to take any toehold on me, Pete thought, although he was displeased at having missed the plate by so far a margin. This time he tried to get it over and the batter cracked it solidly, but right at Halligan, who gloved it easily for the out.

Just as good as a strikeout, and quicker too, Pete thought whimsically.

Pence, the Bells' young pitcher, was the next man up and from his earlier appearances, Pete knew him for no stickman at all. He had only to throw hard. Pence swung tentatively at two pitches, both of them high. Pete thought it was as good a time as any to try his fork ball.

He threw it out of a three-quarter overhand motion instead of sidearm, a fluttering pitch that dropped across the outside corner for a third called strike. Pence watched its progress as though fascinated, then turned and went back to the bench. With a nine-run lead, he was not too much concerned.

The top of the Bells' batting order was a swift left-handed swinger. He took ball one, then dumped a bunt down toward third base. The move caught Deke Holleran by surprise, and Pete too.

The third baseman was far too deep to have a chance, but Pete recovered swiftly. He charged from the mound, grabbed, and threw without straightening up. It was close, but the runner was out.

The small number of fans who remained, hoping for the improbable nine-run rally in the Cats' half of the last inning, applauded noisily as Pete came to the dugout.

"Nice play, Skipper," Holleran said. "Maybe you should have started this game."

"I'll say this, that fork ball sure spooked Pence," Liebman asserted. "He didn't know what to do with it."

"He wasn't any more surprised than I was to see

37

it get over," Pete said. He was pleased with himself, though — not because he had disposed of three not very good hitters, but because he had demonstrated that he was no freak trying for laughs. Anyway, the Cats had broken even on that day.

The visiting team's locker room faced that of the Wildcats across the narrow corridor. At the end of the game, the Cats having gone down in order in the last inning, Pete followed his players into the clubhouse.

Outside the Bells' door, he saw Tommy Clauson talking to a tall, gray-haired man. Something about the stranger's face seemed familiar to Pete, but he could not place him at once.

He nodded to Clauson as he was about to enter the Cats' locker room. The sportswriter reached and grabbed his arm.

"You know Foxy Thurlow, Pete? Foxy, this is Pete Conroy."

"A pleasure, Foxy," Pete said and shook hands as recognition arrived. No wonder the man had looked familiar. Though he had never met Thurlow before, Pete remembered countless pictures of the Cardinals' 25-game winner of 15 — or was it 20? — years ago. Twice winner of three games in a single World Series, strikeout record holder, indeed a memorable name in baseball history.

"Foxy's out here looking over a couple of the Bells," Clauson explained, and Pete recalled that the once-famous pitcher was now a scout for the major-league Eagles. Bellview was one of the Eagles' farm teams.

"Some of them looked pretty good to us in that second game," he said with a rueful smile. "Particularly that kid Pence."

Thurlow said in a husky voice that the young southpaw was a good prospect. "I was interested to see you out there on the hill in the ninth," he remarked with a quizzical look. "I didn't know you'd ever done any pitching. How long have you been trying it?"

Pete laughed. "Since day before yesterday. We've got a couple of sore arms and I thought I'd try saving manpower. All I do is get the ball over if I can."

"Really?" Thurlow seemed surprised. "Well, you throw it hard, which is natural enough. But what was that you threw Pence for strike three? It acted something like a knuckler."

"I'd say it was a nothing ball," Pete said, blue eyes twinkling. "Technically, I guess it was a fork ball. Joe Michaels showed me how he threw it, and you know how everyone fools around sometimes. I've done it for a couple of years."

"It might be worth something if you can control it," Thurlow said. "Nice to meet you, Conroy — you too, Clauson. I have to catch a plane. Maybe we'll see you back in our league one of these days, Conroy."

"Thanks, I sure hope so," Pete said, trying to sound enthusiastic. It was difficult, for he had the

impression the Eagles' scout was merely being po-
lite.

The only big league games I'll see will be those
I pay to see, he thought, suddenly quite depressed.

Nor was the grayness of his mood lightened by
the knowledge that he had to write a report for
Joe Metz about some of the Wildcats, including
Halligan.

CHAPTER 4

"FLEMING HAS PERFECT DAY: HORNETS WIN."
Pete Conroy, scowling, laid down the Winston *Register* and concentrated on the scrambled eggs the waitress had put before him. The Actor had hit all around the circuit — single, double, triple, and home run — and was undoubtedly the most widely discussed player in the league at that moment.

The big hot dog, Pete thought acidly, and his expression was so sour that the waitress, passing by his table, stopped, concerned.

"Are the eggs all right, Mr. Conroy?"

"Pardon?" Pete was wrenched from his thoughts. "Oh, yes, everything's fine."

She gave him a look of uncertainty and went on her way.

Everything was not fine at all, Pete reflected morosely. For one thing, it was going to be another scorcher of a day; a shimmer of heat was already rising from the pavement at 11 o'clock in the morning. For another, he had an appointment in half an hour with Bill Simpson, the Wildcats' president. Pete had no idea what was on Simpson's mind.

He had found the president, a wholesale grocery merchant who had been elected by the other Winston stockholders, rather impressed with his own importance as head of the club.

Thus far, Pete had evaded any discussion of field strategy with Simpson, although he sensed that the man was bursting with ideas on how a ball club should be managed. Joe Metz, however, had made it clear to Pete that, while he should be tactful about listening to suggestions from the team owners, he was the man in charge on the field.

What was also not fine was Pete's memory of the game of the previous night against Northwood. The Cats had lost it because Deke Holleran, playing third base, had gummed up a hard-hit grounder that meant the ball game.

That Pete was pitching when it occurred had nothing to do with his present gloom, he assured himself in all honesty. To be sure, the next hitter had slammed one of his deliveries for a single, driving in still another run, but if Holleran had made the routine stop, the game would have been over.

In the two weeks since impulse had sent him to the mound against Vernon City, Pete had elected to relieve on four subsequent occasions, each time with increased confidence.

He had always been aware that he could throw hard, but that in itself was not unusual for any ballplayer. Some could throw harder than others, that was the only difference. But Pete had also discovered that he could throw accurately, that his sidearm cross fire was particularly effective against right-handed batters and that the three-quarter-speed fork ball with which he experimented as a change of pace broke down and away from right-handers.

I might be a whale of a pitcher — in Class C, he reflected.

Even with his growing confidence, Pete had been careful to pick his spots, relieving in the late innings when the game appeared irretrievably lost or comfortably won, but with the Wildcat pitcher showing signs of distress.

This situation had developed more often than he would have liked, in spite of the opportunities it offered to him as a pitcher. Johnny Hale, unable to work the soreness out of his arm, had been sent home for possible treatment, and the Hornets had not yet provided a replacement.

Of the rest, all youngsters with less than three years' experience, only Bassett and Kavic had shown consistent ability to go nine innings. Robertson, with as much natural ability as either of those two, was as temperamental as a goat, blowing up if a mistake was made behind him or he got what he thought was a bad call from the plate umpire.

Luke Bosler was the fourth Winston starter — at least on paper, leaving Dave Elias and Kit Randall, both with control trouble, as the relievers. However, Bosler was erratic and seldom able to finish a game. With Hale gone, the Wildcats were simply short-staffed.

"Well, as long as Joe Metz knows what we're up against," Pete consoled himself. "He knows we can't win the pennant with what we have."

It was, he admitted, a good hitting club, with Hostett at first, Mike Hearn in center, and Pete himself banging away over .300, fifty points better than he could have hoped for with the Hornets. The fancy figure did not delude him into thinking he had blossomed as a slugger, but he saw more fat pitches in Class C than he had upstairs.

Halligan continued to make errors at crucial moments. The outfielders threw to the wrong base or tried for shoestring catches on balls they should have let bounce, and vice versa.

These were largely mistakes of inexperience, and other teams in the league made them too. But Pete found them galling.

"I'm not cut out to be a manager," he decided. "I simply don't have the patience."

Halligan in particular seemed to be developing something of a martyr's attitude under Pete's criticism, but Pete had orders to use him every day and help him learn his trade, since he was so highly regarded.

Though Pete did not realize it clearly, most of his impatience stemmed from the fact that he could make the plays that his own men could not, and not merely from memory, as was the case with older managers retired from active duty. He made them every day, at third base, second, or shortstop. It was one of the compensations of playing regularly. He had not missed a game since the season began.

In relieving the floundering Randall in the eighth inning on the previous night, Pete had taken on a game that he had privately conceded to Northwood. The score in the top of the eighth was 9—4, but the Cats exploded for six runs in their half of the inning, and Pete began to waver in his decision to pitch the ninth, a decision he had reached as Winston started its turn at bat.

The big blow was a bases loaded homer by Hearn that put the Cats on top, 10–9. But there was no one warming up in the Winston bullpen when it happened, and Pete did not want to risk further arm strain by a cold pitcher. His own arm was limber enough from throwing the ball around the infield.

He decided to stick it out and would have made it too, even though a walk and a bloop single put Northwood in position to score the tying and go-ahead runs. They wouldn't have scored if Holleran hadn't stepped on his hands trying to pick up the ground ball.

The Wildcats maintained a club headquarters in a downtown office building. Simspon, a thin, nervous-looking man given to sudden jabbing gestures to bring home a point, greeted Pete with a querulous expression.

"Say, Pete," he began, aiming a forefinger, "how come you've gone in to pitch so often recently? You got some idea you want to change positions? Or is it some kind of gag?"

Pete's blue eyes glinted in annoyance. The question did not irritate him as much as Simpson's brusque manner, as though the man were talking to one of his grocery clerks. But he was aware that he was in the presence of his nominal employer.

"Neither," he answered mildly. "Our pitching hasn't been very reliable, we're one man short, and the hot weather takes something out of them. Besides, I've gone in only when it looked as if the game was settled, trying to avoid using a regular for an inning or two. These kids aren't effective if they have to come back the next day."

"I know, I know," Simpson said testily. "I'm not trying to tell you how to run the club, Conroy. But take last night, for example. Holleran dropped a ball, so we lost. I think you would have handled it if you'd been playing third instead of pitching."

Simpson's reasoning struck Pete as so illogical that he could not restrain a broad grin.

"What's so funny?" the president demanded. "I don't see anything humorous about losing."

"Neither do I," Pete said hastily. If Simpson was so obtuse that he could not see the flaw in his own reasoning, Pete decided it would be painful to explain. He might have been playing third base, to be sure, but that didn't mean the situation at the time would have been identical or that the particular ball Simpson was talking about would have been hit toward third.

"I'm not saying you haven't gotten by with this pitching kick occasionally," Simpson said. "But you have to agree that we'd have been better off last night if you had stayed at third base."

If I had stayed at third and let Randall stay in, Pete thought in exasperation, Northwood might have had 15 more runs.

He did not say that to the Wildcats' president, but on the other hand, he was not going to let Simpson run him off the mound.

"I can't agree entirely, Mr. Simpson. The hope is that our pitching will get better so that I won't be needed in relief."

Simpson harrumphed and said he understood the Wildcats' problem, and added petulantly that he was certainly going to write Joe Metz about it. Pete left, outwardly composed but seething inwardly.

The truth was that the idea of becoming a pitcher, or at least trying it, had begun to grow on him. He had become reconciled to the fact that he had only a slim chance to work his way back to the majors as a utility man. Dixie Fleming had seen to that.

Pete did not doubt that he could be of value to a minor league club in a tougher league than Class C. But to know that one would always be a minor leaguer at Pete's age was a frustrating outlook. Harry Hall was an example of that.

No, if he were going to get back in the big circuit, it must be at a job he hadn't tried before. Managing wasn't one, he conceded. That left very few available — only one, in fact.

And why not? he asked himself. He was young

47

enough to learn. He had not mentioned it in his communications with Joe Metz, but certainly the farm chief, who saw the box scores of every Winston game, was aware that Pete had gone to the mound more than once in recent weeks.

When Johnny Palmer, the Hornet scout whose specialty was looking at young pitchers, came to Winston, Pete hoped he would have the opportunity to put himself on display. In the meantime, Bill Simpson could go soak his head.

"Hey, Skipper, how do you throw that gizmo you use now and then — you know, the fork ball?" Clem Bassett put the question to Pete as the Wildcats warmed up before the game that night.

Pete, playing catch with Chuck Hostett, paused, and asked with a smile, "Are you serious? You don't need that pitch, with your stuff."

"No, honest," the right-hander said earnestly. "Liebman says it's a dandy when it breaks right."

"He does?" Pete was quite pleased to hear that. "Well, it's a secret that's been in our family for years, handed down from father to son, but as a special favor I'll show you."

He demonstrated how he gripped the ball, and Bassett studied it carefully.

"Are you going to try it?" Pete asked.

"Sure, why not? Harry Hall keeps telling me I need a change-of-speed pitch to go with the fast one."

"O.K., Clem." Pete sounded dubious. "But don't throw this thing with the bases loaded, please?"

48

How about that? Pete thought, amused. Me showing somebody how to throw a trick pitch.

He wound up elaborately and threw it to Hostett, who returned the ball with a big jug-handle curve, as much as to say, anyone can do it.

Robertson went the full nine innings that night for the first time in his last six efforts, but the Wildcats lost, 3–2, on one big inning. Halligan, still showing a trace of timidity when making the pivot at second with a runner trying to break up the double play, threw wide, and the batter was safe.

Robertson took the throw from Hostett after the play with a snapping motion to show his displeasure and Pete felt like taking the pitcher by the shoulders and shaking him as he might a sulking child. He refrained, fuming, because Robbie had been pitching well until then, and Pete didn't want to upset him further.

A walk and an infield out moved the runners to second and third, and both scored on a single between third and short that skipped under Pete's straining grasp. As he ran out toward left field to take the relay throw, too late to catch the second runner at the plate, he felt sick at heart. It was the kind of ball he would surely have gloved a year ago, he thought. But he had been unable to get the jump, the quick start he needed.

His thin features were pinched with the realization of defeat as he walked slowly into the clubhouse, just in time to see the glowering Robertson kick viciously at a wooden stool. It spun half a

49

dozen feet, narrowly missing striking Liebman in the leg.

"Hey, take it easy!" the big catcher protested.

"The best game I've pitched all year!" Robertson spat out. "What do you have to do to win one?"

Silence fell on the other players at the pitcher's outburst. Pete's eyes hardened and he reached Robertson's side.

"Hold the phone, Robbie," he said curtly. "I know it was a tough one to lose, but don't take it out on the furniture."

"Ahhrr." Robertson made a strangled noise of disgust, gave Pete a sullen look, and sat down in front of his locker, staring at the floor and making no move to get out of his uniform.

Pete stood irresolute, then turned abruptly and went into his own small office. Once inside, he regretted not calling out Robertson when he had the opportunity. Temperament was one thing, but temper tantrums were something else, and he should have demonstrated to all the Wildcats that he would not tolerate them.

The trouble was that he did not feel on firm ground, because he still felt he should have stopped the grounder that drove in the deciding runs.

I can't field and I can't manage, he thought bleakly.

The Wildcats left on a road trip next day and Pete faced it with less repugnance than usual. Traveling by bus and eating in small, charmless hotel restaurants could be an exhausting experience, but it was an inescapable feature of life in the lower minor leagues.

This time the trip had a certain appeal. None of the owners accompanied the team.

The Cats opened with three games at Bellview, including a doubleheader with the temperature in the 90's.

Pete chatted briefly with Maury Andrews, the Bells' veteran manager, on the sidelines before the first game.

"You can turn off the heat any time now as far as I'm concerned, Maury," Pete remarked with a grimace.

Andrews pretended astonishment. "Wha-a-at? This is nice and refreshing, man! You want it hot, wait till you come back here in August."

"I'm looking forward to it," Pete said.

Kavic started the first game and went four innings, followed by Bosler, with Elias finishing. None pitched badly, but the heat took its toll of each. The Bells used two pitchers and won it, 6–4.

"Mother told me there'd be days like this," Fuzzy Deraine said with a wan smile as he sank back against his locker between games. "Any chance of calling off the second game, Skipper?"

Pete said lightly that he did not think the cash customers would approve, but he was inwardly concerned. He had seen weather of this kind drain well-conditioned athletes of their stamina. He would not have minded sitting out the second game himself, but rejected the temptation. It would hardly be fair to the other regulars.

"Hey, Pete, come take a look at Kit. He doesn't feel good."

The Cats' trainer tugged at Conroy's sleeve and he went quickly to Randall's locker. The pitcher, his face pale, was sitting down, holding his head in his hands.

"He's a little nauseated. The heat, probably," the trainer said. "I don't think he ought to go out to the field."

From Randall's appearance, it was obvious he shouldn't. Pete told him to return to the hotel and go to bed.

"If you feel any worse, call a doctor, Kit," he advised. "I'll check with you as soon as I get back."

The team stayed in the relatively cool dressing room until the last possible moment. Pete went back to the field with a thin furrow of worry on his brow. Clem Bassett was pitching the second game and if he got into trouble, either Bosler or Elias would have to take over again after each had pitched in the first game. Robertson couldn't be called upon with only two days' rest, after pitching nine full innings.

Bassett did not get into real trouble. His control was imperfect, but his pitching was effective. He got behind the hitters frequently, and although he succeeded in retiring the Bells scoreless through the first four innings, during which he struck out seven of them, he went to a three-and-two count on several.

Eventually, he simply wore out in the sweltering heat.

Although not as sharp in his control as Pete had seen him, Bassett's fast ball was humming and his breaking stuff was good. He even threw the fork ball two or three times for strikes, an accomplishment that delighted him.

"How'd you like that one, Skipper?" he called after a batter had watched the lazy-looking delivery drop over the outside corner. "That's a great invention of yours."

Pete had to smile, particularly since the Wildcats had jumped to a 3–0 lead in the first inning and increased it to 7–0 in the top of the fifth. But he felt a growing anxiety about Bassett, because he was aware that the right-hander was using a great many pitches. He strolled to the mound as the Bells prepared to bat in the fifth, and asked Bassett how he felt.

"I'm fine, just fine," Clem answered, but Pete noticed that his upper lip was beaded with sweat.

"You're going great, boy, but don't work any harder than you have to on a day like this. Concentrate on getting that first one over. They've been laying back on it."

Pete disliked the idea of telling a young hurler to ease up, even with a big lead, but Clem was apparently trying to strike out every man. Under similar circumstances, a major league hurler would be content to get the ball over the plate, but there would be a major league defense behind him, too.

Bassett began by walking a batter, struck out the next one, and then yielded two singles and a run before the side was retired. Pete drew Liebman aside as Bassett bent over the water cooler.

"He looks as if he's starting to aim the ball, Gus. I've got half a mind to take him out right now."

The catcher agreed that Clem was laboring harder than he should with a 7–1 lead, but thought he might get by.

Pete singled and scored behind hits by Hearn and Hostett, and the Cats led 9–1. But Bassett had a shaky sixth inning, walking two batters and giving up two runs. Twice Pete went to him to give him a breather and urge him to throw strikes. At the rate Clem was going, he would throw 150 pitches or more in nine innings, and Pete knew that was simply too many in such dehydrating conditions.

Clem slouched off the mound after the third out, exhaustion obvious in every step. Conroy made his decision at once. He told the pitcher to hit the showers. Bassett objected, but not strongly. Then Pete beckoned Harry Hall from the shadows of the dugout.

"Come on, Harry, let's throw a few."

The catcher groaned. "I like it here, Pete. It's the only cool spot in town." But he picked up his mitt and followed Pete down to the bullpen.

"You figuring on turning pitcher one of these days?" Hall asked with a grin.

"It's an idea," Pete answered shortly.

"I was wondering. Luke and Dave only worked a couple innings; they could go again."

54

"You let me do the managing, eh, Harry?" Pete said, and Hall's lips compressed in a thin line.

"Sure," he said sullenly and retreated to the bull-pen plate. Pete was irritated as much by the catcher's attitude as by the realization that Hall was right. Bosler or Elias could be called on for the three innings necessary. But he, Pete Conroy, had his own reasons.

I might need both of them, he thought wryly, if the Bells start clobbering me.

But the Bells did not clobber him. He felt more at ease on the mound than at any time before, particularly since Winston picked up three more runs in the top of the seventh to make it 12–3 before he delivered his first pitch.

With that margin, Pete simply wound up and fired, relying on the fast ball almost entirely, throwing the change of speed just frequently enough to keep the hitters from timing the fast one and setting themselves for it.

As a result, they were swinging late most of the time and frequently hitting the ball on the ground. Pete did not try to strike them out; he concentrated on keeping the ball low and near the plate. He gave up one hit in three innings, did not walk a man, and permitted only two balls hit out of the infield. Both were flies that were easily caught.

"Hey, nice going, Skipper," Liebman yelled. "That fast ball was really dropping in."

Pete tried to conceal his pleasure. "Ah, I was just trying to let 'em hit it," he said with a shrug. "What I was trying to get Clem to do."

"Clem doesn't throw as hard as you do," Liebman said.

"Come on, what are you pulling? A little of the old oil?"

"Not at all," Liebman protested with a pained air. "Sure, he's got more stuff, but he doesn't overpower 'em, like you did."

Pete gave the catcher a searching look. The youngster seemed quite sincere, and there was no reason why he should try to flatter the manager. He was already the number one catcher on the club and obviously destined for higher status no matter what Pete might report about him.

Well, now, Pete thought, exhilarated. Come and take a look, Johnny Palmer. Come any time.

CHAPTER 5

JOHNNY PALMER was a long string bean of a man, younger in appearance than his 42 years might indicate, clear-eyed, and the picture of health. Until five years ago, the Hornets' chief scout had been one of the craftiest left-handed pitchers in the business. When his arm lost its zip, he joined the Hornets' front office, without trying to get by in the minors.

He uncoiled from a chair in the lobby of Winston's best hotel as Pete came through the doors.

"Hello, Pete," he said pleasantly. "Hope my call this morning didn't wake you. I imagine you got in fairly late."

"Not too bad this time," Pete said with an answering smile. "We finished in a hurry last night, for a change — hour and 58 minutes. Kavic was sharp; walked only one man. So we got an early start out of Northwood and were home before one o'clock. I had just finished shaving when you called."

"Good. I'll stick around for two, maybe three, days, but I thought we might get together before you went out to the park. Had breakfast?"

Pete said he had, but that he could stand a cup of coffee, and Palmer led the way into the hotel coffee shop.

"You had a pretty good road trip," Palmer said.

"Five out of nine. We hit well, thank goodness. Our pitching is still shaky, but I imagine you know all about that."

Palmer grimaced. "It's a standard complaint. The Hornets could use another reliable starter, as who couldn't? If it weren't for the way Fleming's been going, we might be in fourth place instead of second right now. Wait till the doubleheaders start piling up; every team will be crying for help."

Mention of The Actor brought a scowl to Pete's forehead. Palmer looked blank for a moment, then made a little move with his hand that might have been an apology.

"I forgot, Pete. You're not one of Dixie's rooters, are you?"

"Should I be?" Pete could not keep the bitterness out of his voice. "Ah, let it ride, Johnny. It was an accident."

The scout, anxious to divert the conversation into other channels, said quickly, "I particularly want to get a look at Bassett this trip. When will he go again?"

"Let's see. Tomorrow night. If you stay that long, you'll probably see the whole bloomin' staff."

"Including you, I understand," Palmer said with a tolerant smile. "You've been playing fireman now and then, I see. Just for kicks, I suppose?"

Pete ran a hand nervously through his black hair. This was his first opportunity to dispel the assumption that his efforts on the mound were some sort of joke.

"No, not for kicks, Johnny," Pete said, his eyes intent on the scout's face. "When I first tried it a month ago, it was a spur-of-the-moment affair because we were in such an awful jam for relievers. Since then, though, I've gone in maybe six, eight times and have done pretty well, if I say it myself. You can check our box scores on that, Johnny. I can throw hard and I get the ball over. That's a beginning, isn't it?"

Palmer seemed to be lost in his own thoughts. "Yes, you always did have a whip, Pete," he said after a moment. "Am I to understand that you want to make the switch to pitcher, or what?"

"I'd like to give it a real try," Pete said, as eager as a schoolboy. "I don't mean pitching exclusively, but when there's a need for it. At least until I see if I have any future in it."

Palmer grunted. "Well, it's not impossible, I suppose. The Cincinnati Reds had a real good pitcher 20, 25 years ago named Bucky Walters. Came up as a third baseman and played there about five years before he changed over. He helped the Reds win a pennant and a World Series, if I remember right. But he's the only one I can remember who had any success.

"Frankly, Pete," he went on, frowning slightly, "it's not up to me to tell you yes or no. That's Joe Metz's job. Naturally, if you turn out to be a

59

nugget as a pitcher, the Hornets won't let you go to waste. But being able to throw hard and get by for a couple of innings in this league is no real test."

"I'm not stupid enough to think it is," Pete said doggedly. "But how else will I find out?"

Palmer laughed and held up his hands in mock surrender. "O.K., O.K. Go ahead and find out, then. As a matter of fact, I'd like to see you work, but don't force it. Fair enough?"

Pete said it was, and the talk turned to other Winston players. Pete learned that Palmer had an appointment with Bill Simpson that afternoon.

"The difficulty with these working agreements, especially in a league like this one," the scout said, "is that you run into situations where you have to decide between leaving a player with one club because he's valuable to it or moving him up to a higher league where he might be even more valuable.

"Take yourself for an example, Pete. Austin could use you right now, but Joe doesn't want to mess around too much here. Confidentially, he'd like to send Bassett up to Bay City if he looks ready for it. But if he pulled you out of Winston, too, the owners would howl and I couldn't blame them."

Pete's lips parted slightly in astonishment. "Me go to Austin? That's news to me. What would they do with me up there?"

"Shortstop, mostly. They've had trouble."

Pete was more than a little dismayed. The possibility of his own move to Austin could not be considered entirely as a promotion. It implied also that he was less than satisfactory as a manager. But if he did stay at Winston, the loss of Bassett would be catastrophic.

"If you take Clem away," he protested, "you'd better replace him in a hurry. Either that or figure on the second division — if we're lucky. We still haven't got anyone to take Johnny Hale's place. Are you aware of that?"

"I am, and so is Joe Metz," the scout said. "We'd like to make a good showing here, but there are other teams in the organization that have to make a showing too, remember that, Pete. Let Joe handle it."

Palmer sat behind the Winston dugout that night and watched the Wildcats beat Garfield, 9–7. Kavic received credit for the victory, though needing help from Randall.

Pete had a poor night, making one bad throw that cost a run and going hitless in five trips to the plate. He was grateful enough for the victory, but the information he had received from Palmer had upset him. The prospect of going to Austin was not alluring. It was in a Class A league, only two jumps away from the majors, but it was likely to be the last stop for a utility man not quick enough to make the big play. It might be a living, but it offered no future.

Unless you were a pitcher, Pete added to himself.

It was a shame, he thought the next night, that

61

Clem Bassett had to pick that game, with Johnny Palmer looking on, to turn in his first poor performance in a month.

But poor it was, and when the Garfield second baseman, not known as a long-ball hitter, drove one out of sight with two men on in the seventh, making the score 7–2, Pete gloomily waved Elias in from the bullpen.

He did his best to console the downcast Bassett. "Tough luck, Clem, but all pitchers have a night like this every so often and you were overdue. What was that Engle hit — the change-up?"

"Fork ball," Bassett said unhappily. "It didn't break, just hung up there."

"Oh," Pete said. He could think of no other comment.

Elias retired the next man to end the inning, but even as Dave came to the box, Pete had made up his mind that he was going to pitch the last two innings.

Elias was the second man up in the Wildcats' half of the seventh, and it was sound strategy to pinch hit for the pitcher in the hope of starting a rally. If a rally did not develop, Pete could logically defend the choice of himself to succeed Elias on the mound rather than use another member of the bedraggled Wildcat staff in a game apparently lost.

Even if it weren't defensible logically, he was determined to let Palmer see what he could do.

Unfortunately, what he did first was to hit Keller, a right-handed batter who led off the Garfield eight, right between the shoulder blades with his first pitch, and drop him writhing in apparently terrible pain at the plate.

It was the sidearm cross fire, and Pete was aiming for the outside corner, with no intention of even trying to brush Keller away from the plate.

The only explanation he could arrive at later was the possibility that he somehow released the ball sooner than usual. At any event, it acted as though it had been aimed behind the batter before it started to break.

Keller, instead of attempting to avoid it by dropping to the ground, turned his back and tried to fall away from the plate. The ball struck him with an audible thump and he went down as Pete ran toward the plate.

The Garfield manager, Tim Mahoney, also charged down from the third-base coaching line, arriving together with Pete as Harry Hall and the umpire bent over the stricken player, rolling from side to side in the dirt.

Keller stopped thrashing around at that moment and sat up, face contorted and shoulders hunched. He glared balefully at Pete as his manager helped him to his feet.

A wave of relief swept over Pete and his taut features relaxed. Keller obviously was not seriously injured, although he might have a tender area in his back for a while.

"Sorry, Carl," he offered lamely. Keller continued to glare, but assured Mahoney he could stay in the game, and walked slowly down toward first, trying to reach the stinging spot in his back and rub it.

As Pete turned back toward the mound, Mahoney said in a low, growling voice, "If you're gonna be one of those headhunters, Conroy, you better stay where you are. We got pitchers can throw at you too."

Pete stopped abruptly, all feeling of regret at the incident vanishing at the threat. "Cut it out, Tim," he said, bristling. "The pitch got away, that's all, and you know it."

"Oh, yeah? Well, take a tip from me, sonny. Hitters expect to be brushed back now and then, but they don't like pitchers throwing behind 'em, see? Some of 'em might get real sore at it."

The umpire's brisk, "Let's get going," made further exchange with Mahoney unfeasible at the moment. Pete went back to the box, boiling mad at the implication that he had deliberately tried to hit Keller and at the threat of retaliation.

He was so much occupied by this jumble of thoughts that, as he faced the next batter, he completely forgot that there was a runner on first.

He studied Harry Hall's signal, but instead of turning into the stretch position, bent forward, rocked, and swung back into a full windup.

Hall leaped up from his crouching position and yelled, but it was too late to do anything about Keller. Sore back and all, he had streaked for second on Pete's windup, and the catcher did not attempt a throw. He asked for time and trotted out to Pete with an overly tolerant grin.

"Take it easy," he advised. "Don't let your hitting Keller get you jangled."

Pete felt sheepish about his forgetfulness, but Hall's manner, which struck him as one of sly enjoyment, grated on him.

"O.K., I drew a blank," he said. "Don't worry about it."

"Remember, Johnny Palmer's watching," Hall said with a knowing wink before he returned to the plate. Pete glowered at his back. He knew where Palmer was — right behind the Wildcats' dugout.

A few minutes later he was wishing the scout was somewhere else. Before he could get the side out, he had walked a batter, and allowed a long double to center that drove in two runs.

Of all the games to watch, he has to pick this one, Pete thought in frustration as he came to the dugout, carefully avoiding a glance in Palmer's direction. The Keller incident had unsettled him for a moment, but he could not blame his ineffectiveness on that alone. He had missed the corners with his best pitch and when he did get it over, the batter had swung and hit it. That was all there was to it.

He selected a bat from the rack and went to the on-deck circle as Hostett stepped into the batter's box. The first baseman grounded out, and Pete faced the pitcher, a young southpaw named Griswold, wondering if Mahoney had ordered his hurler to throw at Pete's head.

He found out quickly, for the first ball came

whistling at the spot his chin would have been had he not backed away swiftly.

He wasn't kidding, Pete thought grimly, picking up a handful of dirt and rubbing it on the bat handle. Orders or not, young Mr. Griswold needed a lesson in the facts of baseball life. One of those facts was that the batter had certain opportunities to strike back at a headhunting pitcher.

High and tight, low and away, that was a familiar pitching pattern. Pete hoped for a low outside pitch and got it. He shortened up on his bat and pushed a bunt down the first-base line.

The first baseman was too far behind the bag to have a chance at the ball; Griswold was the only one who could make a play on it.

To get to the slow roller, he had to scramble down off the mound in a hurry and come almost into the base path down which Pete was racing. The pitcher grabbed it, straightened, and reached out to make the tag, as Pete hoped he would.

Griswold had one foot inside the three-foot lane that was the runner's strip by right, into which any fielder came at his own risk. Pete made no effort to evade the tag; instead, he lurched slightly to his left, catching Griswold in the chest with his shoulder and knocking him off balance. The pitcher staggered backward and sat down, but retained his grip on the ball.

Pete was out, but he had the satisfaction of seeing Mahoney pop out of the Garfield dugout, yelling and gesticulating at the umpire as Griswold got to his feet a little shakily.

As Pete pulled up past first base and turned to come back, the first baseman said out of the side of his mouth, "Playing a little rough, aren't you, Conroy?"

Pete gave him a stony stare but did not reply. If he had wanted to play rough, he could have used his spikes on Griswold instead of giving him the shoulder. This was a mild warning to the rest of the league that he didn't mind being pushed back from the plate and would overlook an errant delivery that was unintentional, like the one that had hit Keller, but that he would not hold still for a deliberate beanball. There was a difference.

The incident, however, did nothing to improve his control in the ninth. He struck out the first batter with the fork ball, as it dipped away prettily nearing the plate. But the cross fire was coming wide to the right-handed batters and he walked two of them before a hard line smash right at Deraine was turned into an easy double play. Two feet higher and the ball would have gone for extra bases.

He took some consolation from the fact that Garfield hadn't scored in the inning, but he knew he had not dazzled anyone. Maybe he had followed through too much on the sidearm, Pete thought. He had been conscious of the need not to release the ball too soon, to avoid repetition of the pitch that had hit Keller. Probably he had compensated for that too much.

The Wildcats picked up two runs in the ninth and the game ended 9–4. Johnny Palmer was sitting on a rubbing table in the clubhouse, swinging one leg rhythmically, as the Wildcats trooped in.

"Not much to cheer about tonight," Pete remarked glumly.

Palmer shrugged. "Everyone has a game like it now and then, sometimes oftener. I did notice that Bassett was using some kind of half-speed pitch — the one they hit the homer off. Looked like one you threw a few times, Pete? What was it?"

"It was the fork ball — good a name as any. He has done pretty well with it, though. The one they hit just hung up high."

"Fork ball, eh? Is that where you picked it up —from Clem?"

Pete hesitated. "It's the other way round, Johnny. He got it from me."

Palmer stopped swinging his leg as though an invisible hand had clutched it.

"*You* showed him?" he demanded incredulously. Pete nodded and the scout looked as though he had been informed that a four-year-old child had built a television set.

"Look, Johnny," Pete said apologetically, "it wasn't my idea. The kid saw me trying it and asked about it. He's been using it on his own."

"I'm glad to hear that," Palmer said with a sigh.

"Joe Metz would go straight up if he thought you were trying to monkey with one of his good young pitchers."

"And while we're on the subject, Pete," he added gently, "do yourself a favor. Don't spoil a good all around ballplayer with strange ideas. You understand me?"

Pete's heart sank. "You're talking about my pitching, I suppose."

Palmer nodded.

"I can pitch better than that," Pete said pleadingly. "I have pitched better; you can look at the records. Do you usually make a decision on only one look, Johnny?"

"Not if I see anything there to begin with, Pete. You didn't show me a thing tonight to warrant a second look at your pitching. Be practical. You're a young man and you've got plenty of good baseball ahead of you. You do a lot of things well. Why toss them away for something you don't do well?"

Pete took a deep breath. "I won't admit I can't become a pitcher — not yet," he said doggedly. "Anyway, what harm can it do if I try? I pick my spots; we haven't lost any games we might have won with someone else pitching."

"Maybe not. But if you're concentrating on that, it isn't going to help your batting or fielding, particularly when you have the responsibility of managing the club, too."

"Johnny, are you ordering me not to pitch anymore?" Pete demanded in a low voice, shaky with emotion.

The scout looked at him coldly, lips compressed. "I've told you, it's not my job to give orders, just advice. Take it from there."

He slid off the rubbing table and went across the room to talk to Clem Bassett, leaving Pete seething with indignation. He felt he had been dismissed like an errant child, and on insufficient evidence.

That's a piece of advice I'm not going to take he vowed silently, glaring at Palmer's back.

That was before advice became a direct order.

CHAPTER 6

THREE DAYS after Johnny Palmer had departed from Winston, the order came at eight o'clock in the morning, when Pete was dreaming blissfully of striking out Roger Maris.

The insistent ring of the telephone eventually aroused him. He groped groggily for the instrument by his bed, mumbling imprecations against the uncivilized lout who would make a call in what seemed to be the middle of the night.

But he came awake quickly at the faraway sound of the telephone operator's voice.

"Mr. Peter Conroy? Just a moment; long distance calling. Go ahead, please, Mr. Metz."

"Conroy!" Metz's voice was loud enough for Pete to understand at once that the Hornets' farm chief was not making a pleasure call. "What in blazes are you trying to do there? You're supposed to be running a ball club, not a toy factory!"

Pete, still trying to chase the remnants of sleep from his mind, was too stunned to make an immediate answer.

"I'm — I'm trying to do my best," he got out finally.

"It doesn't look that way from the report I have

here," Metz said in a high, rasping voice. "You're supposed to help those kids learn something, but you've got Halligan so mixed up he doesn't know which way to move. And what's this pitching bug you've developed? You're no pitcher, Conroy, and heaven knows you're not a pitching coach. So don't go showing anyone trick deliveries, do you mind? If you want to be a pitcher, experiment when the season's over, not when we're trying to make a decent showing and get some ballplayers out of it, too! You got that?"

Pete, hand clenched on the receiver, could not get any words out at once.

"Conroy? You hear me?" Metz barked.

"I heard you, Mr. Metz," Pete said woodenly, his spirits leaden.

"Well, now, Peter," Metz said in a more cordial tone, "we know the situation and we're aware that you could use another pitcher, but we don't want to send you someone just to fill out a uniform. You'll get one soon, and he'll be what you need. We like the way you've been hitting the ball; keep it up. And, Conroy—don't ride Halligan too hard. O.K.?"

"O.K.," Pete replied dully.

"Fine. I'm glad we've got everything straightened out."

Pete heard the click of the receiver and replaced his own in its cradle. Then he threw back the covers and sat on the edge of the bed for a while, head propped in his hands and a look of hopeless misery in his blue eyes.

Johnny Palmer had really fixed him up, he re-flected. He did not question the scout's motives. Palmer had sent back a report of what he had seen, and Pete granted that it was accurate as far as it went.

Maybe he wasn't handling Halligan in precisely the right way, although Pete remained convinced that the Hornets were overestimating the young-ster's potential. It was true also that Pete was not a pitcher, and viewed from the outside, there was a certain absurdity in the young hurler picking up an unorthodox delivery from a utility infielder.

But it was grossly unfair of Palmer to write him off as a pitcher on the basis of what he had seen. Every pitcher in the game had bad innings on occasion.

It seemed to Pete that an iron barrier had sud-denly dropped in front of him. He had no place to go above a certain level, and he could look for-ward, at best, to being shifted around from team to team in the Hornets' farm system only as an-other minor league utility man.

Even worse, he thought bitterly, would be the frustration and doubt that would plague him al-ways. Could he have become a successful pitcher, or was he, as Palmer implied, only a strong-armed third baseman with delusions of grandeur? Even knowing that Palmer's judgment was correct would be better than the lingering uncertainty.

At the moment, Pete could see no escape from the squirrel cage. He belonged to the Hornets and he could play only for them or their affiliated teams unless he was traded or sold. He doubted that there was a great demand for flat-wheeled infielders.

He sat on the bed, bleary-eyed, tousled, and unhappy, while an automobile being driven on a freeway half a continent away blew a tire and plunged off the road. Three occupants were injured, none seriously. The Winston *Register*, limited in space for news, carried no report of the accident next day, and Pete did not learn of it until many days later.

Had Pete been aware of it, he could not have seen how it would have the remotest connection with him. So he arose and walked like a tired man to the task of toothbrush and razor. He stared bleakly at the face that confronted him in the mirror. It was not a happy image.

Nor did the events to come make Pete's outlook much happier. Rockland followed Garfield into Winston and swept a three-game series, and Northwood stopped long enough to take two out of three, climaxing the Wildcats' poorest home stand of the season. They fell to fourth place in the standings.

There was nothing mystifying about the slump to Pete, who could only grit his teeth and try to bear it without losing his self-control.

The Winston batters, who had been carrying the team despite the indifferent pitching and erratic play afield, suddenly stopped producing. It was that simple.

Chuck Hostett, Mike Hearn, and Gus Liebman, the Wildcats' most consistent hitters, all went sour in the same week. So far as Pete could see, none was swinging any differently than he had been. There was no hint of a hand-hitch or a change in timing, although Liebman, after getting only one hit in twelve trips to the plate, became over-anxious.

"You're reaching for bad pitches, Gus," Pete advised him earnestly. "Don't press. Take your natural cut at the ball and the hits will start dropping."

Liebman admitted that he was pressing and going after balls he shouldn't. He continued to do so just the same.

Hostett's average actually did not drop very much, but the first baseman could not hit when it counted. In the second Rockland contest, which the Cats lost, 7–3, he collected two hits, both bases-empty singles when two were out. Twice he came up where a hit meant two runs and would have put Winston back in the game, and twice he popped up.

As for Hearn, the center fielder, he was more the victim of bad luck than of anything else. He hit the ball hard, but there always seemed to be a fielder directly in its path or making a sensational play. Hearn began to brood about his bad luck, and that did not help him, either.

The strain of managing a team in a losing streak began to show in Pete's playing too. He heard himself booed by the home fans for the first time after he had misplayed a routine ground ball.

Luke Bosler won the only game of the home stand and that was a struggle all the way. The following day, Northwood took the series finale, 15–4, in a display of baseball Pete would have liked to erase from his memory forever.

He was not to enjoy that merciful privilege at once, though. Hot and disgusted, he entered the clubhouse to find Bill Simpson, the club president, pacing nervously up and down.

"Pete, what's the matter with the team?" Simpson demanded in a petulant voice, loud enough for everyone in the room to hear. "Another week like this one and there won't be anybody coming out to see us."

Pete's blue eyes blazed and he controlled a wrathful retort only by great effort. "Let's talk about it over here, shall we?" he said in a low, tense voice, inclining his head toward his office. He could have swung at Simpson. Certainly the man had a right to ask questions, since his money was involved, but the stupidity of sounding off in front of the entire team outraged Pete. The players' morale was low enough at the moment without their being bombed by a grocery magnate.

Simpson stalked into the room ahead of Pete, who shut the door.

"Mr. Simpson," Pete began in a cold voice, "I feel as bad about this as you do, and so does every player. We haven't been hitting when it counts, that's all. It happens to other teams, and they pull out. So will we. There's no reason to panic."

"Who said anything about panic?" Simpson demanded heatedly. "I represent the people who have money in this team and they're worried. Some of them wonder whether we're getting the most out of the players we do have. They certainly can do better than they have been. You'll admit that, Conroy."

Again Pete wrestled with his temper. "If you have any suggestions on how to start them hitting again, I'd be delighted to hear them," he said with exaggerated formality.

Simpson flushed. "Don't get sarcastic with me, young man," he said, jabbing a forefinger at Pete. "You're the manager, and frankly, I don't think you're doing a very good job of it."

"If you're dissatisfied, why not write to Dan Ricketts?" Pete exploded, making no further effort to mask his anger.

"I may do just that," Simpson said ominously and walked out.

Pete tore off his cap and was about to hurl it against the wall, anything to relieve his smoldering fury at the club president. But he held on to it instead, let his arm drop limply to his side, and sank into a chair, all his nervous energy suddenly spent.

Ricketts isn't going to listen to that donkey about how to run a baseball team, he thought wearily. The Hornets' owner would probably write Simpson a conciliatory letter and let it go at that.

Unless Simpson could think up a way to keep Liebman from swinging at bad pitches.

Again Pete welcomed the chance to get out of Winston, if only for a few days — a three-game stand at Vernon City, two at Bellview. Slumps did not last forever and perhaps the change of scenery would help.

It did, to a certain extent. The Wildcats won the opener at Vernon City, 11–7, as Liebman hit a tremendous home run and Hostett drove in five runs with three hits. But the home team chased Kavic early, attacked Elias savagely, and Randall had to finish up.

That, Pete hoped, signaled the end of the batting slump, and he was right. However, it proved a two-way street, for the Vernon City swingers showed little respect for Winston pitching. Bassett, the victim of poor support, went the distance to win the second game, 9–6, but the final contest of the series lasted 13 innings before the home team won it, 10–9, Randall, the fourth Wildcat pitcher, walking in the winning run.

Pete hit well and fielded errorlessly in the series, but he could not dispel the dreary sense of futility that had set upon him since his telephone conversation with Joe Metz.

Yet professional pride overrode his uncertainty about his future, and he entered each game as though it were the deciding contest of the World Series. He derived the professional's satisfaction from any winning effort.

The first thing Pete did upon arriving in Bell-

78

view was to check the sports page of the local paper to see who would pitch against the Wildcats in the first game. He discovered that a right-hander named Carlson had been nominated.

Glad we don't have to go against Pence right away, he thought. The Bells' southpaw had been tough against Winston.

He glanced causally over the rest of the page and Pence's name leaped to his eyes in the heading of a separate story.

"The Eagles yesterday recalled Bellview pitcher Stan Pence and assigned him to New Bristol of the Class A Northeastern League. Pence, 20, has won nine while losing two for the Bells so far this season."

Pete was faintly surprised that the Eagles had moved the youngster up so quickly. Still, he conceded, Pence was a fine prospect and might possibly cut it in the higher league, although Pete thought that a full season in the Central Plains circuit would have taught the pitcher a great deal.

The Wildcats gathered in the hotel lobby before boarding the bus to the ball park. Pete was counting heads when he saw Foxy Thurlow come out of an elevator and toss his room key on the hotel desk.

The Eagles' scout caught sight of Pete as he turned and walked over to him with a cordial smile.

"Hello, Conroy. How goes the battle?"

"Not too bad. We've started to hit again. For a while we weren't."

"Those things have a way of evening up," Thurlow said. "What about your pitching?"

"I've seen better," Pete said ruefully, and Thurlow laughed.

"I meant you in particular. Are you a regular reliever these days?"

"Oh, that," Pete said, his good humor evaporating. "I'm afraid that's all over."

"How come?" Thurlow's brows arched. "I had the impression you were doing pretty well. Maury Andrews told me you mowed 'em down the last time you were here."

"Joe Metz didn't care for the idea," Pete said in clipped tones and sought to change the subject, a painful one.

"I see you've sent Pence up to New Bristol. Can't say I'm sorry we won't have to look at him anymore. Is that why you're out here again?"

"Partly." Thurlow grimaced. "Naturally, when you bring somebody up, you have to replace him. The Eagles had to take Grossman from New Bristol; that's why Pence went there. I've been on the move since the accident, seeing what I can find to help out the big club."

"Accident?" Pete was mystified. "What kind of accident?"

Thurlow looked at him in wonderment. "Didn't you read about it? I thought it would be in every paper. It happened last month. Blaney, Emmerick, and Haines were riding in the same car when it blew a tire and turned over. I suppose they're lucky all of 'em weren't killed."

"I hadn't heard a word about it, Foxy," Pete said, appalled by the news. "Were they seriously hurt?"

"Serious enough. Blaney broke his leg, Emmerick busted two ribs, Haines got a fractured wrist. They'll be all right eventually, but we can't figure on any of them for the rest of the season. We might get Andy back, but the others, no hope."

Pete knew Andy Emmerick as the Eagles' shortstop and field captain. Gordon Blaney was a starting pitcher, and Haines a reliever. Loss of them would be a terrific blow, but his immediate sympathy went out to the players.

"What a rotten break!" he said in a shocked voice.

Thurlow agreed grimly that it was all of that and departed, leaving Pete meditating on the whims of fate. Three good men knocked off a pennant contender in a mishap that apparently had been unavoidable. Not like the one that had brought him to his present state, he thought, with a flaring of his old bitterness. He hoped the three Eagle players would prove luckier than he in that respect.

He could not rid his thoughts of the accidents, the Eagles' and his own, even at the ball park. They both impressed him as needless waste, and his features mirrored his gloomy frame of mind so obviously that Gus Liebman was prompted to inquire.

"Something bothering you, Skipper? You don't look very happy."

"Don't I? Well, I'm not," Pete answered sharply. Liebman looked puzzled and a little hurt.

The Wildcats' performance that night did nothing

81

to dispel Pete's depression. Robertson got only one man out before the home team had three runs, and Pete reluctantly waved in Kavic, whom he had hoped to start the next day.

Kavic pitched well enough through the sixth, but the Wildcats could do nothing with Carlson and trailed 6–1 going into the seventh.

Kavic was scheduled to bat third, Pete noted, and that meant a pinch hitter if the Cats had even a single base runner at that time. If there were two outs and no one on, however, Pete was inclined to let the pitcher hit for himself, saving his relief staff and hoping that Winston could get something going in the last two innings.

He looked down toward the bullpen, where Elias and Randall were resting. Both pitchers had worked almost every other day for the past two weeks, including the previous night, and Pete knew they were both tired.

Fuzzy Deraine led off the inning with a clean single and Halligan drew the first walk Carlson had issued. That meant bullpen action and Hall scrambled to his feet at once.

Pete stood immobile for a moment, undecided. Then he turned abruptly to the dugout and pointed to Gary Pelter.

"Get a bat and swing for Larry, Gary. Deke, you'll play third."

The last was directed to Holleran, in the third-base coaching box. Pelter selected a bat as Pete trotted toward the bullpen.

Pete's spur-of-the-moment decision was not motivated by any wish to defy Joe Metz's instructions. The Wildcats' pitching staff was overworked and ineffective to boot; they were still waiting for the help the Hornets had promised.

If Metz wants to know why I'm pitching, I'll tell him we didn't have anyone else and that's the truth, Pete thought darkly.

Harry Hall greeted him with a quizzical look. "Going to try it again? I thought you were all through with this stuff."

Pete, about to reply that this was purely an emergency measure, froze. He had been under the impression that only Palmer and Metz were aware of the order to forget pitching. Apparently Hall knew of it too.

"Where do you get your information, Harry?" he demanded frostily. Hall seemed flustered, for he walked down to the bullpen plate without answering.

Pete was indignant at the idea that Palmer had made a confidant of Hall, and his mood was not made any lighter by the sight of Pelter, the pinch hitter, grounding into a double play that snuffed out all chance of a big inning.

Although he had time for only half a dozen tosses to Hall before the third out, Pete's arm felt loose after he had completed his preliminary throws to Liebman from the mound.

He was also mad clear through — mad at Hall, Palmer, Metz, Simpson, the whole Hornet organization, and Dixie Fleming too. He bent forward for

Liebman's signal, scowling as though the batter were his deadly enemy.

Some of his anger seemed to flow into his arm, for he was not only swift but accurate. He knew he was facing the tail end of the Bellview batting order, not a powerful array, but he might have been pitching to Mickey Mantle, Willie Mays, and Frank Robinson for all the attention Pete paid to them as individuals.

Relying only on the sidearm cross fire against the first hitter, who swung right-handed, Pete struck him out on four pitches, the last two called strikes. Against the next batter, a left-hander, he went to a three-quarter overhand delivery, but his control was still near perfect and he got his man on an outside fast ball that was popped up to Liebman. The third man, Carlson, looked at three hummers and retired without taking a bat off his shoulder, in the tradition of most pitchers at the plate.

The Wildcats scored two in the top of the eighth to make it 6–3. Pete, somewhat exhilarated by his command of his fast ball, set the Bells down in order in their half of the inning, one on an infield fly, two on the fork ball breaking down and out, which both hit into the dirt.

Winston did not score in the ninth.

Wonder what Johnny Palmer would have said if he'd seen me tonight? Pete asked himself with a trace of bitterness. No future?

His future became known to him sooner than he had anticipated.

CHAPTER 7

THE WILDCATS came home from Bellview to the luxury of a day off before the series with Garfield. They were now only a half game out of fifth place, and even Tommy Clauson of the *Register* was prompted to write a "What's wrong with the Cats?" piece.

It was a legitimate question, Pete reflected ruefully. At any rate, Clauson had not put the exclusive blame on the manager. He wrote quite bluntly that the Hornets did not seem to be much concerned with turning out a winner at Winston or they would have done something by now to bolster the pitching staff.

Pete smiled as he read that. Joe Metz wouldn't care much for Tommy's column, if he happened to lay hands on it.

The telegram was waiting for him at the ball park when he arrived the next evening. It was short.

"REPORT AUSTIN MONDAY LATEST. TRANSPORTATION BEING SENT. BE AT HOME PHONE 9 A.M. TOMORROW.
　　　　"(Signed) JOSEPH C. METZ."

Pete Conroy went into his small office, shut the door, and laid the piece of yellow paper on his desk. He could not truthfully claim complete surprise, but he was undeniably shaken.

Austin, he thought dully. A faster league, but still a dead end.

He folded the telegram and shoved it into his coat pocket, then mechanically began to undress and get into his playing clothes.

As he pulled his flannel undershirt over his head, he heard the sound of voices outside. The Wildcat players were arriving and he thought suddenly, Am I still the manager?

The day was Thursday and he could not leave Winston until after Metz had talked to him next morning. He finished dressing quickly and went into the locker room, now filled with players in varying stages of undress.

"Hi, Skipper," Holleran waved at him. Liebman grinned amiably at Pete as he surveyed the room. There was nothing to indicate that any of them had heard of his impending departure.

At that moment Bill Simpson, accompanied by Harry Hall, came into the locker room. Simpson looked a bit startled as he caught sight of Pete, standing there with hands on hips.

"Oh, Conroy," he said, flustered. "Glad you're here."

Where did he think I'd be? Pete asked himself sourly. On a plane to Austin?

Hall, standing behind Simpson, ducked away toward his locker, and Simpson called, "I'll see you later, Harry."

Then the president inclined his head toward Pete's office. "Can we talk for a moment in private?" he asked.

He seemed somewhat embarrassed as Pete closed the door.

"I suppose you know by now that the Hornets have recalled you and are sending you to Austin. They feel they need you more there than here."

That isn't the way I'd put it, Pete told himself, but he masked his bitterness with an air of stolidity.

"I had a wire from Metz telling me about it. Who's taking over this team? Harry Hall?"

"Well — yes, as a matter of fact, he will be the manager," Simpson said, flushing slightly. "You understand, Conroy, the change hasn't been officially announced yet. It has to come from the Hornets' office tomorrow. Naturally, they wanted to inform you in advance, and of course, as president, I was entitled to know about it before it's given to the newspapers."

"You mean the players don't know about it?"

"Not yet," Simpson admitted uncomfortably. "Only Harry and I. Until tomorrrow, when it's official, you're the manager. I thought it might save some explaining."

"Good," Pete said briskly. "Then I'd better get our lineup posted in the dugout."

He sat down at his desk and began writing names on a card, a move that Simpson correctly interpreted as one of dismissal. The president fidgeted, started to say something, then went out without a word.

As the door closed, Pete stopped writing and sat back with a brooding look on his thin features. His mind was still a jumble, and he had not yet had time to assay the significance of the telegram now reposing in the coat that hung in the closet opposite him.

But he knew that he would have difficulty keeping his attention fastened on the duties of a third baseman as he mulled over what the future held for him. As the official manager, he would give himself a night off for the first time this season and direct the field activity from the third-base coaching box while Holleran patrolled the infield corner. And Harry Hall could do the catching.

Pete's absence from the list of starters, tacked on the dugout wall, drew instant reaction from the players as they studied it.

"Hey, Skipper, are you sick?" Mike Hearn asked with a show of concern.

Pete said he wasn't, and with an outward show of good nature that he did not feel, parried similar questions with the explanation that he merely felt like resting. If that struck some of the players as odd, he did not care. He was not going into details.

Clem Bassett and a Garfield southpaw named Fowler hooked up in a neat pitching duel through the first seven innings. It was 2–2 when Fowler weakened in the eighth and put men on second and third with only one out.

Halligan was the Wildcat batter, and for a moment Pete considered going to the bat rack and substituting himself for the young second baseman. But he decided against it. Halligan would think he was being persecuted again.

Let him strike out for himself, Pete thought resentfully.

Halligan did not strike out. He lined a single to right to score both runners, and Bassett went out to pitch the ninth with a 4–2 lead.

He walked the lead-off man on four straight pitches. Pete, immediately concerned, and forgetting for the moment that it was no longer his worry whether Winston won or lost, called for time and hustled out to the mound.

Bassett was frowning down at his right hand. "Blamed thing just started to hurt," he said as Pete approached, showing him a blister the size of a dime near the tip of his middle finger.

"For heaven's sake, Clem, have you been pitching with that all night?" Pete demanded in exasperation.

"Oh, no," the young right-hander said innocently. "It started about the fifth inning, but it didn't bother me until now. I can't grip the ball hard with that finger."

"I don't wonder at that," Pete growled and turned toward the bullpen. Elias, Randall, and Liebman had been taking their ease there while Bassett sailed through the first eight innings.

It had been Pete's intention to wave in Elias, but he arrested his arm motion suddenly and spoke to Bassett.

"Go get that looked after, Clem, and have some-one bring me my glove."

Bassett looked surprised, then grinned. "Go get 'em Skipper," he said. "I'm counting on you to save this one for me."

"And, Clem," Pete added as an afterthought, "send for Liebman, will you?"

Harry Hall was at Pete's shoulder by now, mask in hand, and a questioning look on his face.

"Oh, Harry," Pete said blandly, "I'm going to finish up for Clem, and Gus will catch. Go down to the bullpen and get Elias ready, just in case."

Hall gave a little shrug. "In case of what?" he asked sourly and slouched off.

Pete could not deny enjoying his successor's discomfiture, although he had not asked for Liebman out of any malice toward Hall. He simply felt more confident with Gus behind the plate.

But he did have to plead guilty to a kind of small-boy defiance in selecting himself as a reliever, at least in part. In greater measure, though, he was moved to try again because his success against Bellview had made him more determined than ever to test himself further. The more he tried, the more convinced he became that he was not completely deluding himself in the belief that he could become a pitcher.

Gary Pelter ran out with Pete's glove and Liebman hustled down to the dugout for mask and pad as the plate umpire walked out to ask Pete gruffly what was going on.

Pete beckoned Bassett out to show the umpire

his blister, and the arbiter, after examining it, said, "O.K., but don't take all night."

Under the rules, Pete had as much time at his disposal to warm up as he wanted. When a pitcher was incapacitated, either by injury or illness, his replacement could throw until he felt he was ready to pitch.

It did not take Pete long; he had learned he was a quick warm-up. After some 15 pitches, about double the number allotted a relief pitcher under normal circumstances, Pete felt that his arm was limber enough.

Liebman crouched and gave the sign as the first man, a left-handed pinch hitter, came to the plate. Pete came to the stretch position, turned, and threw to first to keep the runner close. He did not anticipate a steal, but the hit-and-run was a distinct possibility. With a left-handed hitter, the pitcher would have the responsibility of keeping the ball inside where the batter would have less chance of hitting to his off-field — that is, through the shortstop. The shortstop would be the man to cover second base on any play to the infield.

Pete shook off Liebman's first sign, waited until he got the signal for the fork ball. If it broke right and went where he wanted it, the batter might hit it on the ground and set up a double play. Besides, Pete had come to think of the delivery as his "get 'em out" pitch, if he ever got the chance he sought.

He stretched, came down, kicked, and threw. The ball came in spinning at the batter's knees and he swung. But it was breaking down toward him and he topped it, sending a roller right at Pete.

Pete was down off the mound like a cat, picked it up, whirled, and threw to second, where Deraine made the stop and threw to first for the double play.

The fans applauded, and Hostett brought the ball over to Pete with a little head jerk of approval.

Pete got two strikes on the third hitter, tried to waste one outside, and didn't get it far enough outside. The batter laced into it and it went a long way, but Mike Hearn was under it when it came down, and the game was over.

Well, Pete thought, as his first apprehension subsided, if that's the last inning I'll pitch, at least it was a good one.

But he convinced himself it would not be his last. Joe Metz was a strong-minded man, but he was not completely unreasonable. Results counted with him.

Pete did not sleep very well that night, for he was composing in silence the case he would present when the phone would ring. He had been awake for two hours when it finally sounded.

"Hello, Conroy," Metz's voice came through strongly. "You got my wire? All right, don't take it hard, will you, boy? This is really a promotion, you know. You're too good a ballplayer to be wasted in Class C. I told Dan Ricketts that from the beginning. You there, Conroy?"

"Yes, sir."

"And I told Ricketts, too, that it wasn't fair to

make a manager out of a youngster with your experience. He agrees with me now. It was his experiment and it didn't work out, but you needn't feel bad about it. Sam Velie is hurting for a shortstop at Austin and we're counting on you to fill the bill. How much time do you need to check out of Winston? One day, two days?"

"Mr. Metz," Pete said, "will I get a chance to try my hand at pitching in Austin? I did pretty well the last couple of times. Even Bill Simpson will tell you that."

Metz did not answer for what seemed to Pete like a very long time. He did not notice how tightly he was clutching the receiver as he awaited the important reply.

"Now listen to me, Conroy," Metz said, sounding like a man reasoning with an inquisitive child, "I thought we'd agreed to forget that stuff. Velie doesn't need pitchers — even good ones. He's got the best staff in the league right now. What he needs is an infielder."

"Mr. Metz," Pete said with a desperate note, "Johnny Palmer saw me only once. Why not let him, or anyone you pick, look me over again before you decide?"

Again there was a protracted silence. Then Metz spoke, in a more conciliatory voice.

"I don't want to appear bullheaded about this, Conroy, so I tell you what. I'll tell Sam to let you pitch batting practice any time you want. Next spring, when the Hornets go to camp, you come along, and we'll take a real good look at you as a pitcher. How does that strike you?"

Pete's spirits had begun to rise at the Hornet chief's first words. Now they plummeted. He knew what batting practice involved — throwing what the hitters asked for, not what the pitcher needed to improve. And he was certain that Metz's aim was to get him to Austin without delay. The "real good look" by the Hornets next spring would probably last one or two days. Then, back to Austin or some other farm club.

The injustice of the bland refusal to give him even a fair trial, as Pete viewed it, pulled the trigger on all the resentment and bitter anger that had been building up in him for weeks.

"No!"

Pete was startled at the vehemence in his own voice, and realized that he must make an effort to control himself.

"No, Mr. Metz," he said, firmly but without sending his voice to a higher register, "no, thanks. I don't want to report to Austin under those conditions. Maybe I'm wrong about being a pitcher, but I think I deserve a better shake on that than I've gotten so far. I'm not going to Austin or anywhere else."

Afterward, Pete reflected that Metz deserved some credit for not exploding. The man had to deal with dozens of minor league players, and one infielder more or less could not loom as terribly important to him. When Metz spoke again, he was cool and indifferent.

"Well, young man, if you won't, you won't. Your travel money ought to be there today. If you change your mind, use it to go to Austin. Otherwise, forget it. You're not playing for anyone else, you know that?"

"I know all about it," Pete said, his face pale beneath his crop of black hair.

"So long as you understand that," Metz said and hung up. Pete sat limply by the phone for a while, still shaken by the significance of what he had done. He had made a decision in the midst of anger, but he knew he would stand by it.

I'll be a lot better off in the long run, he told himself, if I go back to the engineering company. I'll be established in a sound business five years from now and my career will only be starting to open up. If I went to Austin, five years from now I'd still be there or some place like it.

It was a valid conclusion, but Pete viewed it without enthusiasm. He had lived with baseball too long to take leave of it without a wrench.

Yet leave it he did, that afternoon, without the formality of farewells to anyone except Tommy Clauson of the *Register*. He would have liked to say good-bye and good luck to youngsters like Liebman, Bassett, and a few others, but facing the entire team and explaining was an ordeal he chose to avoid. Bill Simpson could do the explaining.

Pete did not wish to face Clauson, either, but he felt he owed the reporter something. He telephoned the *Register* from the airport, 20 minutes before his plane was to leave.

"Pete!" Clauson exclaimed. "I've been calling you for the past hour. We just got the story that you're going to Austin. I suppose I ought to congratulate you, but I don't think it's fair to the Wildcats."

"Don't congratulate me, Tommy," Pete said wryly, and told him why. Clauson listened in astonishment, obviously finding it difficult to believe that Pete was quitting.

"You'll change your mind, Pete. You'll be back playing for somebody, I'll bet on that."

"Don't bet very much, Tommy. Joe Metz is a stubborn man."

Clauson smothered a laugh. "I know it isn't funny, Pete, but it did sound odd. If Metz is stubborn, what are you?"

"Well, since you put it that way," Pete said, "I don't know. Stupid, maybe."

Minutes later, his plane was climbing over the airport. As it circled once before heading west, he looked down and saw the Winston ball park beneath him.

It was too late for regrets.

In his judgment of Metz, Pete Conroy knew it was impossible for the man to send word that he had changed his mind, all was forgiven, and that Pete could pitch for Winston or Austin or wherever.

Yet for a day or two after he arrived home, Pete permitted himself an occasional flight of fancy in which that happened.

Metz did not send word. He was a stubborn man.

Pete did not call on his engineering employers at once. He did not even inform them of his return and it was unlikely they would learn of it from another source. The refusal of a little-known minor league player to report to another minor league team far away was not an item of national importance.

"I'll go in tomorrow," Pete decided after a week's idleness. He had attempted to rationalize his delay by assuring himself he deserved a brief vacation. But he knew the real reason was that once he went to work, a door would be forever shut behind him. He needed time to adjust to that.

Pete Conroy had not overestimated Joe Metz's stubbornness. But he had underestimated him as a practical businessman who would not let spite stand in the way of a profitable transaction.

When the telephone call came, it was not from Metz.

"Hello, Conroy, this is Foxy Thurlow, remember?"

"Of course I remember." Pete felt the excitement rising in him. He was surprised, but he sensed that the Eagles' scout was not making a mere social call.

"Look, Conroy, this is going to surprise you, but the Hornets just traded you to New Bristol for a shortstop. The deal was closed an hour ago and they asked me to call you."

"New Bristol?" Pete asked dazedly. "What — what will I do there, Foxy?"

He heard Thurlow chuckle. "You won't do anything at New Bristol, Conroy, because you ain't even going there. The Hornets don't know it yet, but you're joining the big team — the Eagles.

"The Eagles?" Pete said stupidly. "They need a shortstop?"

"They could use one," Foxy Thurlow said. "But you're not the man. You're coming up as a pitcher, lad!"

CHAPTER 8

FOXY THURLOW met Pete Conroy at the airport. It was raining hard, a midsummer electrical storm against a background of rumbling thunder.

"Greetings," the Eagles' scout said, his face breaking into a smile. "Anyway, you won't have to pitch tonight."

"Tonight?" Pete said stupidly, then looked sheepish as Thurlow laughed.

"That was supposed to be a joke. Let's round up your bags and I'll drive you to town."

Pete said, "I know I'm a little slow today, but honestly, I'm still in a fog over this whole deal. I could use a few details."

"On the way in," Thurlow called over his shoulder as he led the way through the terminal to the baggage-claim counter. That errand completed, they hurried through the rain to Thurlow's car. Foxy sat back for a moment to regain his breath.

"The game tonight has already been called," he said, shaking the raindrops from his hat and running a hand through his curly gray hair. "That's why I made the crack. Say, why don't we go to the ball park first? Meredith is there. I've staked out a hotel

99

room for tonight and you can shop around later. Unless you have other plans?"

"Plans?" Pete asked helplessly. "I don't even know what I'm supposed to do here. Pitch batting practice?"

"That's up to Buzz Meredith," Thurlow said as he started the car. "But the Eagles didn't buy you with that in mind. By the way, do you know Meredith?"

"I wouldn't say I did. Of course, when we played the Eagles maybe he said hello, or how's tricks, or something like that, but I've never had a talk with him. I've heard he's a smart manager."

"He is that. Also a very fair man, but tough if he thinks anyone isn't bearing down. He can also be stubborn."

Pete remembered Meredith as a small wiry man with rather a mild look, but he took it for granted that the Eagles' pilot could be hard-nosed if necessary. Managers who weren't did not last as long as Meredith had, in the big leagues.

Thurlow drove out of the airport and swung the car onto the freeway. He began to talk against the soft, rhythmic squishing of the windshield wipers.

"I'll start at the beginning, Pete. Bringing you up is a long shot, but it's an insured long shot. We're gambling you'll make a pitcher, but if we're wrong, we've still got a utility man who could be mighty useful in our system — with a club like New Bristol, for example. That's our insurance."

"I see," Pete said. The difference between Austin and New Bristol was merely one of geography

100

if it turned out he was not a pitcher but only a fielder who could not make the big play.

"I imagine you're the man responsible for the gamble, Foxy," he said, and Thurlow nodded.

"I suppose I am, although you have to put part of it on Paul Gordon, the club vice-president. Once he was convinced you were worth a shot, it was easy."

"And you convinced him?"

Thurlow laughed, a little uncertainly. "I don't know if you'll ever make a pitcher, Pete, and you don't either. I saw you only a couple of times. You impressed me, and Maury Andrews, and a couple of other fellows I asked to take a look at you.

"Maybe it was that big whip of yours, Pete," he went on. "Being an old pitcher myself, I always like to see the man with the hummer. If he has that and control too, he can learn to throw the curve and all the other fancy-name jobs like the slider and the slip pitch and the screwball. They used to be called differently in my day. That thing you use — the fork ball. It may be something new, but I'll bet some pitchers were using it 25 years ago and calling it something else."

Pete said he didn't think Joe Michaels, who had shown him the pitch, had invented it.

"Anyway," Thurlow said, "I remember thinking that with that speed and the big sidearm motion, something like Drysdale's, you might go somewhere if you buckled down to it.

"I was surprised when I heard that Joe Metz had told you to forget it. I figured that you'd sure get a real trial if you were Eagle property, the shape we're in since losing Blaney and Haines. Do you know how many pitchers we've brought up in the past few weeks? Six! And just one of them, Stu Berry, is still with the club. We've lost half a dozen games for lack of a late-inning stopper, so you understand why we're willing to take a chance on you."

"Couldn't you have bought or traded for someone?" Pete asked in all innocence.

"Ha!" Thurlow made it sound like an epithet. "You think a team like the Eagles, with a chance for the pennant, is going to get a helping hand from another contender? The Gold Sox offered us Tom Corla, but all they wanted was Ace Elwood, probably the best young catcher in the league. Anyway, we figure Corla is worth at least four games to us with the Sox. We beat him about that often every season.

"So we had to bring up some of our minor league pitchers, hoping lightning might strike and one of them might win for us. So far we haven't had much luck."

"You think maybe I could be the lightning?" Pete asked.

"Why not? It doesn't happen every day, but they've come up from Class B and made it. No one knows how good you may be. Or how bad," he added. "Unless you think the job might be too big for you?"

Thurlow took his eyes from the road long enough to give Pete a sidelong look. Pete hesitated. He had fought for the chance to pitch, but he had not been prepared to start at the top. It was like throwing someone into the water to see if he could swim.

"I'm like you Foxy," he said frankly. "I don't know how good I may be, or how bad. But I'd sure like to find out."

Thurlow seemed satisfied with the answer.

"Of course, it never occurred to me we'd have a chance to get you. I still don't know the reasons, but when I read that you wouldn't report to Austin, I got on the phone to Meredith right away.

"It took some talking, but we had a young infielder at New Bristol we could spare and thought the Hornets would be willing to unload a player they couldn't use for one they could. As far as they knew, it was a minor league swap of infielders. If Dan Ricketts had any idea he was giving away a pitcher, he might have nixed the deal just on suspicion."

Pete had the impression that Thurlow had been forced to do a lot of selling on him.

"Do you take the rap if I flop?" Pete asked.

"Sure," Foxy said cheerfully. "But it won't be much of a rap. There isn't a scout in the business who hasn't touted more lemons than bananas. Some of 'em have given away thousands of dollars of a club's money to sign some schoolboy who never got within mailing distance of the majors. As money goes, you're a bargain, and as I said, you carry your own insurance. You can always play somewhere."

Pete winced. They were now driving within the

103

city limits and soon he saw the rain-drenched outline of the Eagles' stadium. Thurlow swung the car into the almost deserted parking lot as a weak sun shone wanly behind the gray clouds. The rain had stopped.

Thurlow led the way through the players' entrance to the clubhouse and Pete had a brief whiff of days remembered as they went through the double doors of the Eagles' locker room. Across the hall was an identical set of doors marked VISITORS, though which he had passed several times.

Half a dozen men were in the locker room as Pete followed Thurlow across it to Meredith's private office. All were in street clothes. Two were methodically autographing baseballs, one was writing a letter, two others were listening to a table radio, and one was wandering aimlessly as he sipped from a soft-drink bottle.

"Hi, Foxy," a big, blond man called and Thurlow waved in response but did not break stride. Pete was sure it was Dave Alten, the Eagles' first baseman, although players looked different out of uniform.

The door to Meredith's office was open, and Thurlow walked in without knocking. The Eagles' manager was reading a letter, one of a pile on his desk. He got up and came around the desk to shake hands with Pete. He was a leathery-skinned little man with a long chin and eyes as blue as Pete's own.

"Hello, Conroy. Have a chair. You picked a lovely

day, I must say." He sensed that Pete was not at ease.

"Well, we won't blame you for it," Meredith went on. "I suppose you're a bit surprised to be here, and I imagine Fred Kearns is, too. Not to mention a few others. All thanks to the super salesman, the eminent Doctor Thurlow."

Meredith gave the scout an enigmatic look from under heavy gray brows and Pete received the impression that the manager had reservations about the deal. Possibly he had been overridden by Gordon, the club vice-president to whom Thurlow had referred.

Thurlow said lightly, "Remember Milo Smolich?"

Meredith smiled slightly. Pete did not recognize the name, but assumed it was another player Foxy had recommended in the face of others' doubts.

The manager perched on the edge of his desk and regarded Pete appraisingly.

"I'm told you're real quick and that you can get the ball over," he said, all business now. "We need a late-inning stopper, and since you were brought here to pitch, you'll get a shot at it soon. That suit you, Conroy?"

"Any time you say," Pete said stoutly, although at the moment he wasn't sure he could have put on his uniform straight.

"Good. Now tell me," Meredith said, eyes fixed on Pete's face, "why you didn't want to report to Austin. Was it something personal?"

Pete looked uncomfortably at Thurlow. The scout had not asked him for reasons and Pete could only assume that Foxy did not know them. But the truth was all Pete had to offer. So he spoke it, haltingly and with some embarrassment, but in full detail.

Meredith grunted once or twice during Pete's recital, rubbed his jaw thoughtfully several times.

"Did you know about this, Foxy?"

"Not all of it," Thurlow said, frowning. "But it doesn't make much difference, does it? You're still looking for a pitcher."

The manager again addressed himself to Pete. "Let's say it turns out you won't make a pitcher and never will. What happens if we send you down as an infielder?"

Pete was completely flustered by this time. He had made no false representations, yet he felt like a hostile witness.

"Honestly, I don't know. I don't want to be a minor leaguer all my life, that's all."

"I can't quarrel with that. But I remember you as a real handy andy with the Hornets. I know you got hurt, though I forget how. Then you weren't with them anymore. But you were playing third and short regularly with Winston, so the injury didn't stop you. What did happen?"

Pete told him, in a voice without emotion, concealing his feelings about Dixie Fleming.

"So Kearns thought you had slowed up? Did you agree with him on that?"

"I had to," Pete said frankly. "I couldn't get to balls that I used to reach. There was no sense kidding myself."

106

Meredith nodded sagely. "Kid yourself not, that's a good idea. Well, Conroy, you're here and we'll see. I think Marty Hull, our clubhouse man, is still out there. Maybe he can find a uniform for you. If the rain will let us, we're playing the Gold Sox tomorrow afternoon. Be here at ten and look for Jim Varnell. Foxy, wait a minute; I'd like to talk to you."

Pete went out to seek Marty Hull, a jolly little man about Meredith's height but twice his weight and as round as a beach ball. Hull rummaged through his supply of uniforms and found one that looked promising.

Foxy Thurlow emerged from the manager's office a few minutes later, a brooding expression on his face. Pete followed him outside to the car.

"I had no idea how you felt about playing in the minors, Pete," he said. "I'm proceeding on the theory that you'll make a pitcher, so it doesn't matter. Buzz was a little surprised, that's all."

"I should have spelled it out," Pete said apologetically. "But your phone call knocked me over, and pitching was all I could think about. I suppose it cuts down my insurance, as you called it, but I'll promise this much. I'll finish out the season wherever the Eagles send me and at any position they want. After that, though, I'll have to think it over."

Thurlow said that was fair enough, and put the car in gear. Pete stared moodily out of the window with the feeling that without having thrown

107

a single ball, he had already disappointed the Eagles.

Jim Varnell, standing behind Pete in the fenced-off Eagles' bullpen, said, "All right, Conroy. That's done it for now."

Pete pushed his cap back on his head and wiped his forehead with his sleeve. After the thunderstorm of the day before, the weather had reverted to hot and humid. Twenty minutes of throwing to Ace Elwood in the late morning sun was long enough to bring sweat stains to the white uniform Pete had been given less than an hour earlier.

Pete glanced at Varnell, seeking some expression on the features of the Eagles' gaunt pitching coach that might carry a hint of what he thought after observing Pete perform. But the coach's face told him nothing, nor did that of the pleasant-looking Elwood, the Eagles' first-string backstop. The catcher waited for the other two at the bullpen gate and the three walked out onto the outfield grass, alive with players running down fungo hits, playing catch, or merely running.

The silence was broken by Elwood, who said ominously, "You know, Pete, I'm still sore at you for what you did to me two years ago."

Pete was startled, but before he could ask what he had done to arouse the catcher's ire, Elwood chuckled.

"You jumped about nine feet straight up and speared a line drive off me. I hadn't had a hit in 11, 12 times at bat and when I hit it, I thought it might be good for three. Remember the play? It was at Hornets' stadium in August."

"I guess it's too late to apologize," Pete said. He did not recall the play, but he sensed that the catcher was trying to put him at ease in the face of Varnell's silence. Still, Pete could hardly expect the coach to render a judgment on the basis of 20 minutes in the bullpen.

They reached the Eagles' dugout and Meredith said, "Pete, you hit with the early men and then take a little infield work."

The "early men" were those not in the day's lineup, or who needed extra batting practice. The starters monopolized the batting cage once the formal practice began.

Pete selected a bat and joined the line waiting behind the cage. His introduction to the club had been one of easy informality. Like Elwood, many of the players had been with the Eagles when Pete was with the Hornets. If he knew none of them well, they knew who he was. Even Meredith had called him by his first name.

Pepper Kleeman, one of the coaches, was pitching to the batters, just lobbing the ball over. Pete batted behind Leo Brown, a shortstop, who gave him a friendly nod as he left the cage. Pete lifted two long flies to center field, then jogged out to the outfield to back up the makeshift infield, which had a pitcher on third base, an outfielder at shortstop, and Tad Yerkes, the number three catcher, at first base.

In the shade of the dugout, Buzz Meredith looked inquiringly at Varnell and Elwood.

"He can hum it, all right," Varnell said. "He throws out of third base, a big sidearmer. That's his pitch, although he's got a change-up that acts something like a knuckler."

"That's the fork ball Foxy liked," Meredith commented. "He says it breaks away from a right-handed hitter, a double-play ball. How'd it look to you, Ace?"

"It could be, if he can keep it down. If it gets up high, though, it could be a double home run. But he's fast, Buzz. And he might be awful tough on right-handed hitters in this park for day games. That sidearm cross fire would be coming out of a white background if there's a shirt-sleeved crowd in left field and the batter would have trouble finding the ball."

Elwood pointed beyond third base to the stands, which sloped gradually toward the field until they joined the center field stands on the foul line 340 feet from the plate.

"Of course, he still has to get it around the plate," Elwood conceded.

"Did he show a curve?" Meredith asked.

Varnell shook his head. "I wouldn't call anything he threw a curve," he said dourly. "His fast ball breaks some, but not much. More like a slider."

"Well, see if he can throw one, Jim," Meredith advised. "I want to use him as soon as I can, but I don't want him to get killed. Hey!"

The manager had been looking out toward the

diamond, where Pete had taken over third base from the pitcher, who had been clowning around, ducking away from hard-hit grounders and pretending to wave at others. Meredith's exclamation was evoked as Pete made a backhand stop of a sharp smash down the line, and automatically gunned it to first.

"Conroy just made a nifty grab," Meredith explained to the coach and catcher, whose backs were turned to the field. To himself, he commented, he still has his glove, from the looks of that one. He must have slowed up a lot for the Hornets to turn him loose.

"Say, Buzz, who's the flash at third?"

The question came from a portly, round-faced man in a rumpled suit, who had sauntered over to the dugout by a circuitous route behind the batting cage.

"Hi, Mac," the manager greeted Floyd McGreevy, baseball writer for the *Herald-Dispatch*. "That's Pete Conroy."

"Ah, the great experiment," McGreevy said with immediate interest. "How do you think it will work?"

Meredith's shrug was almost imperceptible.

"I've heard of good hitting pitchers going to the outfield or first base when their arms went bad, but switching the other way is pretty rare," the writer remarked speculatively. "Let me talk to him, will you, Buzz?"

"Sure thing. Hey, Pete — Conroy!"

Pete jogged over to the dugout and Meredith

111

made the introduction. He walked away and Mc-
Greevy sank down on the bench, motioning Pete to
sit beside him.

For the next ten minutes, Pete replied to questions concerning his change from fielder to pitcher
as McGreevy made occasional notes in pencil.

"There are a couple of things I'm not entirely
clear about," the sportswriter said. "Apparently
you pitched well enough at Winston to get a trial
here. Why did the Hornets swap you all of a sudden?"

"They could answer that better than I could,"
Pete replied cautiously, and McGreevy divined that
there was more to the story than his subject chose
to give.

"Another thing I'm hazy about," he said with a
note of apology. "I know you got hurt when you
were with the Hornets, but I can't remember how
it happened."

Again the memory of that bleak day appeared
vividly in Pete's mind, and he gripped the edge of
the bench tightly with both hands.

"It was two years ago," he said in a singsong
voice, like one reciting a memorized piece. "Dixie
Fleming ran into me going after a fly ball. I had
to have a knee operation. It doesn't bother me at all
now."

"Fleming? He's certainly turned into one of the
good ones, hasn't he?"

"Has he?" Pete fought to keep the emotion out of
his voice, and gazed blindly toward the outfield. He
did not want the writer to see the bitterness that

112

he knew was now readily apparent on his features.

McGreevy blinked at the short answer, but said heartily, "Thanks, Conroy, and the best of luck."

He heaved his bulky frame erect and wandered over to the visitors' dugout, where the Gold Sox were gathering.

I'll have to look up the files and check the game where Conroy was hurt, he thought. There was obviously more to that story, too, than he had been able to extract. Part of it, he felt certain, was that Pete Conroy did not like Dixie Fleming one little bit.

But even as he thought about it, McGreevy was putting the idea away in a compartment of his mind as something to be checked in the indefinite future, when this reticent young man would prove worth writing about.

CHAPTER 9

Pete conroy sat in the farthest corner of the Eagles' dugout that afternoon and watched his new teammates beat the Gold Sox, 7–5. No one paid him much attention and he wondered if he might not spend the rest of the season in that same corner.

Pete watched with interest the array of relief pitchers who went out to the bullpen before the start of the game. The bellwether of the flock, he knew, was the veteran Sil De Anza, swarthy and heavy-bearded. Then there was Stu Berry, a young left-hander with a shock of unruly hair and a Southern drawl, called "Rebel" by his mates; Dan Dolin and Duane Smith, both right-handers of some experience; the catcher, Tad Yerkes, and of course, Varnell.

They would watch the course of the game through the bullpen fence until the telephone rang for someone to crank up. On this particular afternoon, that occurred early, for the Gold Sox got to the Eagles' starter, Jack Gregg, quickly, and Meredith hit the telephone in the dugout in the third inning.

De Anza pitched through the sixth, and the Eagles, hitting well, forged in front at 7–3. Smith came in to pitch the eighth. De Anza, the "middle stopper" on the staff, rarely went more than three or four innings. Smith got into trouble in the eighth, but escaped with only one run, and Meredith ordered Mike North, a southpaw who was one of his starters, to go to the bullpen.

North had been elevated to the Eagles' starting rotation after the loss of Blaney, and Meredith's decision to use him as a reliever if necessary emphasized the plight in which Buzz found himself for pitchers.

Still, he's got nine of 'em, Pete thought. He ought to try managing at Winston, if he thinks he has trouble now.

North came to Smith's rescue with one out in the ninth and the batter representing the tying run. He retired the side without further damage, and the Eagles, by virtue of the victory, moved into a tie for third place with the Bengals.

The Generals were in first place, with the Hornets second, and the Chicks fifth, but only six games separated first place from fifth place and the pennant race remained wide open. Expansion of the league to ten teams by the addition of the Robins and the Capitols had not greatly affected the strong clubs.

Pete had been assigned a locker between Elwood and Richie Shipstein, one of the starting pitchers, and as he dressed he listened to their conversation.

115

"If the Hornets lose tonight, we're only a game back of them," Shipstein commented. "Who're they pitching, did you notice, Ace?"

Elwood said he thought it was Guyman and looked at Pete. "Was he with the club when you were?" he asked.

"No, he's new. They've added quite a few players since I left. And got rid of a few, too."

Shipstein said speculatively that the Hornets might be the most improved team in the league. "Since they got Fleming, they've been hard to handle. He gives me trouble, I have to admit."

"They used to call him The Actor when I was with the club," Pete said with studied casualness. "He was good, all right, but some of the fellows thought he knew it a little too much. Is he still that way?"

"Is he?" Shipstein snorted and Elwood laughed delightedly.

"Richie's a little sensitive about Dixie," the catcher explained with a broad grin. "Last time we played the Hornets — well, you tell it, Richie. That is, if you want to."

The pitcher glared at Elwood. "Thanks, pal," he said sarcastically, then shook his head in unhappy reminiscence. "He hit a curve off me — a real good curve, too — and it went into the seats. What does the big hot dog do? He *slides* into home plate!"

Elwood was still grinning. "I thought I'd have to go out and hang onto Richie to keep him from following Fleming into the dugout. Was he steaming!"

"I sure was," Shipstein admitted, but added, with

grim satisfaction, "I knocked him down the next time. Those yokels in the stands went berserk. He's got a neat trick of hitting the dirt on any close pitch, particularly at home, where they think he's the greatest thing since Disneyland. He didn't have to do any acting on the one I threw that time, I'll guarantee you."

"He's even got fan clubs," Elwood said. "Mostly teen-age girls, but it's worth your life trying to get out of the park after Dixie's had a good day. You'd think he was some screamer on television, the way they crowd around the exits from the clubhouse."

The vision of Fleming overwhelmed by autograph seekers was too much for Pete's attitude of indifference.

"I'll bet he takes it big, too," he said contemptuously, and Shipstein looked at him inquiringly.

"Friend of yours too?"

"I wouldn't say so," Pete snapped, and gave his tie a yank to straighten it. He had listened to as much about Dixie Fleming as he could stand at one time.

"Oh, he's kind of amusing, in a way," Elwood said. "You have to give him this, the lad can play baseball."

The next three days for Pete were very much like his first one with the Eagles. He pitched batting practice once, to get the feel of the mound; spent considerable time throwing to Elwood or Yerkes or Charlie Temple, the number two catcher, with

Varnell or Meredith watching; ran with the other pitchers in the outfield; filled in at early infield practice; and then retired to the obscurity of the bench.

Under Varnell's direction, Pete worked on throwing a curve, moved slightly to the right of where he had been accustomed to stand on the rubber and made a slight change in his leg motion.

"You might as well take all you can get with that sidearm," Varnell told him. "But you might try a three-quarter motion, too, for a variation. Keep 'em guessing."

But neither the coach nor the manager gave Pete any hint whether either liked what he saw or was appalled by it. He began to wonder if Meredith had been sincere in saying he would take a look at his new man as soon as feasible.

The fact was that the manager and the coach hadn't the foggiest idea whether Pete could get by.

"I have to use him soon," Meredith said, "or Paul Gordon will be giving me the fisheye. But I hate to risk him in a close game."

"If he can control that crossfire, he's got a chance," Varnell said with a frown. "That's all he has, along with the fork ball. It takes time to teach a man to throw a decent curve and a good change of pace. If he's ever going to make a pitcher, he needs work. Why not send him to New Bristol, where he can get work, instead of keeping him here?"

"Because," Meredith replied with some testiness, "he was sold to us on the basis that he could help

us here and now I owe it to everybody concerned — Conroy, Foxy Thurlow, Gordon — to find
out if he can."

Time and the weather took care of that soon.

The Eagles ended their home stand with a
doubleheader against the Rams in searing heat before a crowd of 40,000. Three Eagle pitchers saw
service in the opener, a free-hitting affair, before
the home team won it, 9–7.

In the comparative coolness of the clubhouse
between games, Meredith approached Pete.

"You go down to the bullpen when the next one
starts," he advised.

"Yes, sir!" Pete said, blue eyes lighting up. At
least it was a start, he thought, though positive he
would be the last man called upon.

Dan Dolin and Duane Smith had pitched four
innings between them in the first game after Bill
Kosecki, the fourth of the Eagle starters, had been
lifted in the fifth. That left Stu Berry and Sil De
Anza, along with Pete, comparatively fresh, but did
not bar the others from duty if needed.

Berry began to complain humorously as soon as
the group had reached the bullpen. He had joined
the club only a few weeks before from the minors,
but he appeared to be an uninhibited youngster,
and age did not awe him.

"Ah wish Ah was back home today," he drawled
plaintively. "Ah could be sittin' under a tree fishin'
for catfish instead of sittin' out in this sun like a
idiot. Duane, why don't they put a roof, or a awnin',

119

or something over this bullpen? Fellow can get sunstroke out here."

"Go on, Rebel," Smith chided. "You can't get sunstroke unless the rays get through to your brain, and as long as you don't get a haircut, the sun has no chance, no chance at all."

"All the same, seems silly to me to fry a man before he goes to work," Berry said, unabashed.

"You serve up another of those high change-ups you gave Beal yesterday," Varnell observed, "and you'll be fishing for catfish, all right. For a living."

"Aw, that didn't do no harm, Jim," the pitcher protested. "Phil Slade got under it, like I knowed he would. It was just a loud out."

The others cackled in delight.

"That reminds me of Lefty Gomez's crack," said Yerkes, the broad-beamed catcher. "Remember, the old Yankee left-hander? Someone asked him the secret of his success and he said, 'Clean living and a fast outfield.' That fits you, Rebel. Half of it, anyway!"

"Which half?" Smith asked innocently. Berry sent him a reproachful look.

Mike North, the southpaw with the overpowering fast ball, pitched steadily through the first five innings as the Eagles pecked away for a 4–1 lead. But he put two Rams on base in the sixth and went to the full count on two other batters before the inning ended. Before it had ended, though, Meredith was on the phone to Varnell, and De Anza and Berry were on their feet and flexing their pitching arms.

"Guess Mike's beginning to feel that heat," Smith observed.

Pete, though resigned to inactivity, was let down a bit, hoping that perhaps the telephone had rung for him. Yet he was pulled in two directions — hoping for the opportunity, but not sure he wanted the first one under the intense pressure of a close game.

But the look of determination on De Anza's face, starting to throw harder as his arm loosened up, reminded Pete that the relief pitcher lived almost constantly under pressure. He was called upon in the threatening situation, and if he could not bear up under that type of strain, he had better try another line of employment.

Like fishing for catfish, Pete thought.

The call for De Anza came quickly, after an error by Leo Brown and a walk had got the tiring North into trouble in the seventh. The right-hander fired one last hard one at Yerkes, picked up his jacket, and went out through the gate Varnell held open for him.

"Pete, you'd better get loose," the pitching coach said as he closed the gate. Pete scrambled erect, pulses quickening. Obviously, Meredith had said something on the phone to Varnell besides asking for De Anza. He began to throw easily to Yerkes, as Varnell continued to warm up Berry.

The Rams sent up two left-handed pinch hitters to face De Anza, but he got out of the inning with only one run scored against him, and as the Eagles prepared to bat, Varnell motioned both Pete and

121

Berry to sit down, an invitation the southpaw accepted with obvious pleasure.

"How many innings you reckon Ah've pitched out here, Jim?" he inquired. "A hunnert, maybe?"

"Out here, you're safe from home runs," Varnell said mildly. Berry chuckled, and Pete saw that the youngster did not mind the sallies aimed at him, even encouraged them.

The eighth inning proved uneventful and the Eagles held their 4–2 lead going into the ninth. The first man to face De Anza doubled to right and after that it was as though a fire alarm had rung among the relievers. Everybody got up, and Ace Elwood rushed down from the bench to help with the bullpen catching.

Pete, already well loosened up, began to fire harder. When De Anza walked the second batter, Berry was on his way.

The Rams bunted, and Stu had to make the play at first, putting men on second and third, with one out. Again the phone rang and Varnell pointed a finger at Pete.

"You ready? You'll be up next."

"Ready right now, Jim," Pete said, pulses quickening.

Meredith came out to the mound briefly to talk to the pitcher and Charlie Temple.

The pitching coach proved right. Berry threw four straight balls to the next Ram for an intentional walk, filling the bases. Again Meredith emerged from the dugout headed for the box, but he was waving toward the bullpen as he moved.

"O.K., Pete, go get 'em," Yerkes said encouragingly. Pete, a little bewildered by the accuracy of Varnell's prediction, started the long walk across the outfield toward his first effort as a major league pitcher.

Varnell had been able to call the shots because he knew from long association with Meredith how the manager's mind worked and what percentages Buzz would play.

With men on second and third and one out, and the Eagles protecting a two-run lead, the risk of putting the potential leading run on first base, as Berry had done, was outweighed by the possible advantages. Filling the bases gave the defense a force play at every base, including home plate, and increased the chances for a double play if the ball was hit on the ground.

Also, Varnell and Meredith were aware that the next Ram batter, a free-swinging right-hander named Claude Marks, would have to face Pete, because the Rams had already used every left-handed pinch hitter on their bench.

Pete did not know this, naturally, as he made the seemingly interminable trek to the infield, past second base to the box where Stu Berry stood disconsolately tossing the ball into the air while Meredith and Temple, a rangy young man built like a football tackle, waited.

Stu handed Pete the ball as he reached the mound, feeling nervousness rise within him at each step. He felt like a man cut adrift. Was he out of his mind, believing he could pitch in the big leagues?

If Buzz Meredith might have been thinking along those same lines, he gave no outward sign. His manner was as calm as though this particular relief pitcher had faced the identical situation many times before.

"This guy is a first-ball hitter, Pete," he said conversationally. "Keep it low and outside to him. Make him hit it on the ground and we can get two."

He gave Pete a light tap and sauntered back to the bench. Temple, guessing at Pete's inner tremors, said confidently, "No sweat, Pete. And don't pay any attention to the man on third, even though he comes halfway down the line. They're not stealing home now. Just give this guy the big cross fire and he won't even see it until it's past him."

Pete gave a little jerk of his head, too tense to say anything. There were 40,000 people watching him and he did not want to make a fool of himself. But he felt a triple kind of fool on his first warm-up pitch.

Exaggerating his wide leg swing in the effort to impress not only the fans but Marks, the batter, Pete was carried slightly off balance as he loosed the ball and slipped off the mound as he followed through. The pitch was so wide that Temple had no chance to reach it. It bounced back against the grandstand as a ripple compounded of amusement and apprehension swept through the crowd.

Engulfed by embarrassment at the ridiculous beginning, Pete kicked with his toeplate at an imaginary obstacle in front of the rubber, as though it were the cause of it all.

Dave Alten, the first baseman, strolled over as Temple was retrieving the wild toss.

"Easy does it, Pete," he advised. "Don't try too hard."

Pete smiled wanly, recalling the numerous occasions on which he, as the Winston manager, had gone to the mound with the same general advice to one of his young pitchers. He had wondered often if his words had any real effect. Right now, he was inclined to doubt it, although he gave Alten full credit for good intentions.

But he finished his warm-up without further misadventure and the plate umpire signaled that time was in. Pete hitched up his belt, pulled down his cap, checked the position of his fielders, reached down for the resin bag behind the rubber, and rubbed the ball vigorously between his bare hands. It was part of the ritual of pitching.

As he stepped on the rubber, he glanced once at the runner dancing off third, took a full windup, and fired. The ball whizzed into Temple's mitt, low and outside, but too far outside. Marks made a tentative half swing, then checked, and it was ball one. The runner from third, yelling "Hey!" as Pete went into the windup, quickly scampered back to the bag.

Pete punched at his glove. He had wanted that one in there to get ahead of the hitter. Temple signaled for the same pitch.

This one went where it was aimed, just above

the knees. But Marks, guessing at the fast ball again, was out in front of it, starting his swing almost before the pitch had left Pete's hand. He tied into it before it started to break, and the ball shot off his bat like a missile.

It was sheer instinct that made Pete leap to his left, reaching as far as he could. The ball struck with stinging force in the palm of his glove, the force of it turning him half around.

Freddie Villa was charging toward second base, screaming for the ball. The runner on second, 20 feet down the line at the sound of Marks's smash, had fallen down in his haste to turn and get back. His fall made no difference, for Pete, like a man in a trance, had all the time in the world to whip the ball to the second baseman for the double play.

As Villa ran toward him with a wide grin, Pete realized the game was over.

"Whew!" Floyd McGreevy slumped back in his pressbox chair and remarked to his colleagues, "As a relief pitcher, I have to say that Conroy is a pretty good fielder."

Much the same thoughts passed through the mind of Buzz Meredith as the pleasure of victory began to calm the nerves so rudely jangled by the sound of Marks's bat meeting the ball.

CHAPTER 10

PETE CONROY read the telegram with a smile. It was from Foxy Thurlow, sent from a small town in the South.

"CONGRATULATIONS."

That was the extent of the message. Obviously, Foxy had seen only the box score and knew nothing of the details.

Jim Grey, the tall third baseman, sauntered past, saw the yellow paper and remarked, "Fan mail already?"

"It's from Marks," Pete said. "He wants to know if I'd like to try that pitch over again."

"He should talk," Grey said. "I'll bet his hands are stinging."

Pete thought that was unlikely, but when you hit a ball as hard as Marks had, swinging from the heels, you felt it. He winced at the memory. An inch or two difference in the flight of the ball and he, Pete Conroy, would have been out of the box as fast as Meredith could get to it.

Instead, he had been enthusiastically saluted by

his teammates, though not for the reasons he would have preferred.

"I don't think I fooled Marks very much," he said ruefully to Ace Elwood when the catcher congratulated him.

"Next time you will," Ace said confidently. "He looks for the fast ball all the time. Change up on him and he twists himself out of shape. You'll see."

Elwood made it sound simple, but a good change of pace was not developed overnight. There was no game on the schedule following the doubleheader with the Rams, but the Eagles had a workout anyway. Pete worked on the change-up under Varnell's observation.

"You have to throw it with the same motion as your fast ball," the coach insisted. "Otherwise, the hitters will read you like a newspaper."

The team departed next day on a challenging road trip that opened with the Hornets, followed by the Bengals, Generals, and Chicks, all first-division teams.

When the Eagles' bus from the hotel backed into the parking lot outside the Hornets' park, Pete knew a moment's nostalgia.

The feeling came again when he went out on the field and some of his former teammates hailed him.

Fred Kearns, the Hornets' manager, stopped in his heavy-footed walk past the batting cage.

"Hey, Pete," he said in a hurt voice, "why didn't you tell me you were a pitcher?"

"You never asked, Fred."

Kearns's eyes twinkled. "I'm glad to see you, and that's a fact. Though I think the Eagles were a little sneaky, the way they dealt for you. We sort of had the impression they were looking for an infielder."

"Is that right?" Pete asked guilelessly. "I thought they had me tabbed as manager material, from my record at Winston."

Kearns snickered, then became serious. "Don't quote me," he said in a low voice, "but they never should have sent you there. You get headaches in jobs like that one that would have driven Casey Stengel off his trolley. You should have gone right to Austin."

"Well, if I had, I'd probably still be there, Fred, instead of here."

Kearns conceded that was true before he continued on his way to the Hornet dugout. After all, it had been partly his decision that Pete Conroy was no longer of value.

Tex White, Willie Gaines, Joe Troyer, and other Hornets stopped to give brief greetings to Pete, whose gaze kept wandering as he sought Dixie Fleming.

He spotted him at last, wandering around the outfield. A long fungo fly was hit to center and as a Hornet set himself under it, Fleming suddenly flitted in front of him, grabbed the ball in a graceful sweep of his gloved hand, and in the same motion flipped it to the surprised fielder.

The same hot dog, only more of it, Pete thought. The Hornets must be used to him by now, though.

Inevitably their paths crossed during the warm-up period. At that moment, had Fleming shown any pleasure at seeing Pete, real or simulated, or said anything to indicate he was glad to see him back in the major leagues, Pete would have buried at least part of the bitterness that had smoldered in him for nearly two years. Anything but indifference toward the man for whose injury he was responsible.

But from Dixie's manner, he might have been seeing some casual acquaintance he had met only the night before.

"Hi, Conroy, how's the boy?" he tossed at Pete as he jogged past him.

"Hi," Pete said woodenly. That was all.

It was not all for Fleming that day, however. He hit a double off Jack Gregg his first time at bat, another in the fifth inning, and made a diving circus catch off Sid Canady, the Eagles' right fielder, that cut off two runs as the Hornets won handily, 8–3.

Fleming was given a fine hand by the crowd each time he stepped to the plate. There was no doubt about who was the most popular Hornet — with the fans, at least.

Pete left the clubhouse in the company of Stu Berry. There seemed to be hundreds of people gathered outside the gate, and the policeman on guard there had to warn them to make way for the Eagles as they headed for the team bus.

As Pete and Berry reached the bus, they heard high-pitched shrieks, looked in the direction of
130

their source, and saw Fleming surrounded by fans waving scorecards to be autographed. Dixie was smiling graciously, his curly blond hair ruffled by the breeze, and was signing as fast as he could. Many in the crowd around him were youngsters, although adults appeared just as eager to get his name on paper.

"Ain't that something?" Berry said admiringly. "If it was up to the baseball fans, that guy could be elected mayor tomorrow."

Eventually, Fleming got through the mob and reached his car, but then he was further delayed by others who milled around and insisted he sign for them too. He seemed to enjoy it immensely. Finally, the police shooed the admirers away from the car, and Dixie drove off.

"Ah wish Ah'd been born talented instead of handsome," Berry said with a mock sigh of regret. "Some people have all the luck."

There was some truth in that, Pete agreed silently.

The Eagles squared the series next day behind Shipstein, 5–2, before a raucous crowd that booed the pitcher loudly after Fleming had dived for the dirt on the first ball thrown to him. His cap went one way and his batting helmet the other.

From the bullpen, Pete could not tell how close to Fleming's head the pitch had been, but Tad Yerkes gave a snort of disgust as Dixie went down.

"That guy is going to start a riot here someday," he said angrily. "If somebody does skull him, they'll come out of the stands."

"You don't think Richie was throwing at him?"

"Naw. Everyone pitches Fleming the same way, high and tight. You pretty near have to. He'll hit an outside pitch against the fence. But when he's on the road, he doesn't flop around like a whale on the beach, the way he does here."

"Still, they do brush him back pretty regularly, don't they?" Pete asked.

"Sure they do," the catcher said. "They do it to all the good hitters, but they're not trying to bean anyone. Shucks, if Richie really wanted to hit him, he would have let him have it in the ribs."

The bullpen corps had an easy day because of Shipstein's mastery of the Hornets, although Fleming did touch him for a grass-cutter single through the infield. The big pitcher was as chirpy as a cricket in the locker room.

Pete joined the other Eagles in offering congratulations to Shipstein on his triumph.

"You see what I was saying about Fleming?" Richie said with obvious satisfaction. "He's always playing to the crowd. Why, that first one I threw him wasn't within a foot of his head! Keep that in mind when you go against him, Pete."

Pete went against him sooner than he had anticipated. It was the very next day, in fact, because the Hornets jumped to a four-run lead off Kosecki in the first inning, and continued the assault against Dolin and Smith.

Pete and Stu Berry had been warmed up for two innings when the Eagles came to bat in the top of the eighth, behind by a score of 9—3. When the bullpen phone rang, Varnell pointed at Pete.

Buzz Meredith made room for him on the bench. "You know something about these guys, I imagine, since you played with them for a while."

Pete said that none of those he knew seemed to have changed much, judging from what he had heard Buzz and Varnell say in the pregame briefing on the opposing batters.

"Well, let Ace call the shots. You throw what he asks for, get the ball over, and everything will be fine," Meredith said. Pete understood clearly that he would be under close scrutiny by the manager, even though the game had already been decided for all practical purposes. This was a "waste look" at him, but it was an important one for him.

Since he had not been following the progress of the Hornet batting order, he had no idea whom he would face in the last of the eighth. But he knew the lineup, and when he saw Chuck Mackey, the leadoff, approach the plate as he warmed up, Pete knew a tingle of expectation. Mackey was followed by Joe Troyer, and Troyer by Dixie Fleming.

Elwood sent the ball down to second base and jogged out for a last word with his pitcher.

"Watch out for this first guy, Pete. He likes to bunt for the hit, especially when he's the first man up."

"I remember," Pete said. Elwood showed fleeting surprise, then understood.

"Now pitching, Conroy, Number 44, Conroy!"

droned the voice of the announcer. Mackey tapped the bat on the plate and took his usual crouching stance. He was a small target, difficult to pitch to, and drew a large number of bases on balls every season.

Elwood called for the sidearm fast ball, breaking in to the left-handed batter, but high enough to minimize the chance of a successful bunt, if that was what Mackey had in mind.

It was. He straightened, shortened up on his bat, and started to run up on the pitch, but ducked away hastily as it swerved in toward him for ball one.

He took a little time to rub dirt on his bat handle and glanced down at Corky Schmidt in the third-base coaching box for the next sign.

"Seems odd to see Conroy out there on the mound," said Kirkpatrick, the Hornet writer, sitting next to Floyd McGreevy in the press box. "He was a hustling little fielder, but I never knew he could pitch."

"The jury is still out on that one," McGreevy answered.

Mackey obviously received the "take" sign from Schmidt, for Pete put the next one right over the middle for the called strike. The next one was low, near the inside corner, and Chuck fouled it off for strike two, removing the bunt possibility.

This was the spot where Pete would have liked to throw the fork ball, and Elwood anticipated him. The big motion and the off-speed pitch caught Mackey flat-footed, for he watched it sail past him unchallenged. The umpire called it strike three, a few fans protested, and Chuck gave the arbiter a look of disgust as he walked away, knocking at the ground with the end of his bat.

Pete took a deep breath, feeling some of the tightness disappear. He had struck out a major league hitter and to him, that was justification for the bullheaded fashion in which he had clung to his belief. At the moment, the fact that the hitter had been looking at his delivery for the first time, with no hint of what to expect, did not matter.

Joe Troyer came to the plate, and Dixie Fleming emerged from the dugout behind him to kneel in the on-deck circle. As McGreevy caught sight of Fleming, he recalled the conversation he had with Conroy from which he had gleaned the impression that Pete did not care much for the outfielder.

McGreevy had not yet gone to the back files for additional information.

"Didn't Conroy run into Fleming and get hurt a couple of years ago?" he asked Kirkpatrick.

"It was the other way around; Dixie ran into him. Conroy hurt his knee and wasn't much good afterward, so they sent him down as a manager at Winston. He's supposed to be a pretty smart ball-player."

"Were there any hard feelings about it?"

"On Conroy's part?" Kirkpatrick looked blank. "Not that I ever heard about, though I don't suppose he mentions Dixie in his prayers. It was one of those things, a mix-up on a fly ball, and Pete got the worst of it, unfortunately."

McGreevy was slightly disappointed. He thought he had stumbled across a story.

Joe Troyer, Pete knew very well, was in many ways the most dangerous hitter on the Hornets in terms of consistency. He "hit the ball where it was pitched," as the players described it. This meant that he had an extremely good eye, did not guess very much, and could hit to all fields, although he did not knock down fences.

But if he was difficult to fool, he could be overpowered, Pete knew, and so did Elwood. Pete whipped across the fast one with as much behind it as he could muster, and Troyer did not even wave at it. He seemed somewhat surprised at Pete's speed, seeing it for the first time, and he shortened his grip on the bat a little more.

The next pitch was intended for the knees, but it came in waist-high, and Troyer lashed at it. He was a little late, and although he met the ball solidly and sent it whistling down toward first base, it was foul by three feet.

Elwood accepted a new baseball from the plate umpire and brought it out to the mound.

"That one sailed, Pete," he said warningly. "Throw at his socks and if the ball comes up, he won't get that much leverage."

Pete, his heartbeat returning to normal after the sound of Troyer's wasted smash, knew why the ball had risen. He had turned his hand over a little more than usual, so that the pitch, instead of being a full sidearm, had almost an underhand twist to it.

136

Whether Troyer expected a waste pitch with a two-strike count or whether he was looking for a change-up after two hummers was immaterial afterward. However, a third fast ball down the slot seemed to find him unprepared, for again he was late swinging and got underneath the pitch, raising a pop fly that climbed in front of the plate.

Pete followed the flight of the ball against the cloudless sky to its apex. As it started to fall back, he judged that it would come down in front of the pitcher's box.

He heard Jim Grey's voice, but stayed underneath the ball, and caught it at his waist.

"Hey, you're supposed to get out of the way," Grey said, a note of sharpness discernible beneath his jocular tone.

"Yeah, you want to get killed?" Freddie Villa asked. "You got no sunglasses."

Pete looked sheepish as he saw that Villa and Bobby Britton, the shortstop, had also converged on the mound. The pitcher usually left such high pop-ups to an infielder, but Pete had gone for it instinctively, forgetting he had no sunglasses to flip down. Fortunately, the sun had already gone down behind the stands.

"I'll remember next time," he promised and turned to face Dixie Fleming, as a round of applause greeted the hitter's appearance.

Pete kept his features impassive as the rangy youngster stood at the plate, bat moving back and forward in a loose, fluid swing.

This is just another batter, Pete told himself,

137

trying to submerge his personal feelings. Pitch him according to orders, high and tight; resist the temptation to hurl the ball with all his force at the handsome, self-assured face; forget that this was the man who put you into the hospital with an unnecessary grandstand play and then shook off all blame for it.

This went through Pete's mind as he leaned forward to study Elwood's sign with a deliberation that caused Fleming to step impatiently out of the box. Pete remained motionless, arms hanging loosely, until Dixie came back.

Fast ball, inside and across the letters, was what Elwood asked for, and that was what he got.

Whether Fleming had guessed at the cross fire or whether he was merely acting, Pete could only conjecture, but the effect was electric. Dixie had stepped into the pitch as though he expected it to break to the outside; he had barely time to realize that it would not and simply dropped in his tracks, losing bat and batting helmet as he did so.

A fearsome roar of boos rose from the stands. Pete's first reaction was one of stunned protest. If Fleming had not tried to move up on the pitch, he could have avoided it by simply leaning back a trifle. In any event, it could not have struck him unless he had stepped across the plate.

Dixie came to his knees and stared at Pete, hands on hips, before he arose. He seemed to be asking plaintively, "What did you do that for?"

Pete took Elwood's throw with a quick flip of his glove and turned his back on the plate, seething inwardly. The outraged yelps from the crowd had jarred him, so much so that he had not noticed what the umpire had called the pitch. He had to check the scoreboard to learn that it was ball one.

Elwood gave him a steadying motion with his mitt before calling for the fork ball. Fleming did not take a full riffle at the pitch, but choked up on his bat, and bunted it down the first-base line. Had it stayed fair, it would have been a hit, for both Pete and Alten were caught by surprise.

But it rolled foul, and Elwood, chasing it down, walked back to the mound with Pete.

"Don't give him anything he can lay down, Pete. Keep it inside."

Pete's reaction to the bunt had been purely mechanical. Now he understood that the catcher was giving him some sort of warning.

"You think he might try it again? The surprise is off it."

"Watch this guy," Elwood said. "He's full of tricks. Dave will play on the grass and Freddie will cover the bag, O.K. If he does bunt, don't get in his way."

Pete nodded assent, eyes glinting at the possibility of a challenge. So the hot dog might try to draw him into the base path, as Pete himself had done to Griswold after the Vernon City rookie had thrown at his head? That was the only construction he could put on Elwood's words, and it suited Pete's mood just fine.

So he wants a little body contact? he thought grimly. We'll see how it comes out this time.

139

Fleming waved the bat in menacing fashion, as though anxious to knock the ball out of the stadium. Elwood signaled, low inside, but Pete was not going to be guided by the sign this time. If The Actor was really anxious to set up a collision course on the first-base line, Pete was willing to cooperate.

He twisted and pitched the fast ball low and on the outside corner, a perfect pitch to bunt. And Fleming bunted it, perfectly.

The ball rolled toward first base. Alten could have made the play with ease, but Pete was down from the mound swiftly as soon as he saw Dixie's hands move up on his bat.

He cut in front of Alten to pick up the ball 20 feet from first base. Fleming was flying ten feet away and Pete had only to turn and lob the ball to Villa for the easy put-out.

Instead he held his position along the base path, partially blocking it, but giving Fleming room enough to avoid contact if he wanted to, but not enough room to evade the tag.

Even though he was prepared for the possible collision, Pete had not anticipated the outcome. He was ready to tag Dixie as he went past, but at the last split second Fleming lunged to the inside.

His shoulder caught Pete in the chest and knocked him over backward like a tenpin. As he lay for a moment fighting to regain the breath driven out of him, he could think of only one thing. That was to get his legs back under him and finish what Dixie Fleming had started.

CHAPTER 11

Fleming caught the ball on a short hop as though in one motion he seemed to be throwing it. The good American League play rotor to an adjacent to the gate. The ector was

PETE CONROY came to his feet with the assistance of Dave Alten, who had one big hand under his arm. His face fiery red, Pete tried to wrench loose, like a panic-stricken drowning man fighting with his rescuer.

"Whoa!" Alten said. He clamped both arms firmly around Pete, who continued to wriggle in the big man's grasp.

What he would have done if left unhampered was not precisely clear in Pete's confused mind. But he wanted to get close to Dixie Fleming, and not to inquire about his health.

Fleming's health appeared to be in question at the moment, judging from the cluster of Hornets around him as he lay on the ground near first base. He was clutching his left shoulder as he rolled from side to side.

Ace Elwood and Freddie Villa raced up to assist Alten in restraining Pete, but it was not necessary. Partly because of the pressure of Alten's thick arms, partly because his initial surge of fury was receding, Pete stopped straining.

He was aware of a roaring sound, and it took

him a moment to realize that it was not inside his head. The fans seemed to be booing as one person, a deep-throated ominous rumble.

"O.K., Dave, you can let go now," he said.

Alten dropped his arms. Pete took a deep breath, and winced. He felt the area on his chest where Fleming's shoulder had caught him and found it sore to his touch.

"Are you all right, Pete?" Elwood asked. "You got rammed pretty good."

Dave Alten said, "The guy who rammed him doesn't look too fancy right now, either."

Dixie was on his feet, holding his shoulder and grimacing. Fred Kearns, the Hornets' trainer, and teammates still hovered about him. Kearns jawed at the first-base umpire, pointing toward first base. The umpire shook his head in emphatic disagreement.

Buzz Meredith materialized at Pete's side and took a firm grasp on his elbow. "Let's everybody get off the field," he said in a rasping voice, with an undertone of urgency. "The inning's over."

Pete cast one more look in the direction of Fleming, still standing near first base and exhibiting signs of pain. He allowed himself to be led to the bench, Alten and Elwood flanking him on either side. He felt like a prisoner being marched off to jail.

As they neared the dugout, the boos seemed to come at them like breakers on a beach. Pete saw some spectators behind the dugout standing and yelling through cupped hands. He could not make out what they were saying, but from their attitude, he assumed it was not complimentary.

"Are they booing me?" he asked in surprise once they had gained the shelter of the dugout.

"Who else?" Meredith retorted curtly. "Looks like you might have wrecked their big wheel."

"I wrecked *him!* He had plenty of room to go past me!"

"Sure, and you had plenty of time to get him at first instead of trying to tag him. What were you thinking about?"

"It seemed easier to put the ball on him," Pete said, not without a sense of guilt.

"You were taking the chance he'd knock it loose, too. You've been around long enough to know that, Conroy."

"I didn't think," Pete said sheepishly. He was being rebuked for a mistake in judgment, but not, he thought, for inviting a possible collision.

"Well, don't 'not think' again," Meredith said. "Go on in. Hey, did you get hurt?"

He flung the last at Pete as an afterthought. Pete touched his chest and said he might have a slight bruise. Meredith told him to have the trainer look at it, and turned toward the field.

Pete ducked into the tunnel that led to the locker rooms as a renewed noise of angry jeers filled the stadium. He could not know that it followed the loudspeaker announcement that Hardy Clampett was now playing center field for the Hornets in place of Dixie Fleming.

He submitted to the examination of the trainer,

143

Casey Adams, who dismissed it as a bruise, no more. Not until he was under the hot shower did Pete sort out his thoughts to realize that for some reason, The Actor had elected to challenge him head on, and that he, Pete Conroy, had pitched a scoreless inning in the majors.

Exhilaration enveloped him. He had come off better than Fleming, judging from Dixie's antics. And although Pete was the aggrieved party in their previous relationship, it was Fleming who forced the issue today. From Elwood's words, Pete judged that Dixie frequently used the drag bunt as a maneuver to intimidate a pitcher who had knocked him down.

But he knew I hadn't tried that; it wasn't that close, Pete thought in mystification, then gasped as he turned the shower faucet and needles of cold water stung him.

As he toweled himself, he wondered what damage Dixie had actually sustained, if any. He might still be acting, Pete told himself uncharitably.

The question was also a matter of interest in the press box. Ken Kirkpatrick got on the phone to the Hornets' dugout and reported that, although it was too early to be sure, Fleming had apparently not broken anything. This evoked expressions of relief from other Hornet writers, plus querulous demands to know what the pitcher was doing in the base path.

Floyd McGreevy, a puzzled look on his fleshy face, said, "What was your man doing, bunting with two out and nobody on? Especially after he'd missed once. I don't get it."

"He's very fast," Kirkpatrick replied. "He's done it before, but I don't know why he ran into the pitcher. Maybe he stumbled."

"Uh-huh," McGreevy mumbled and noted in his scorebook a single for Phil Slade, the Eagles' lead-off in the ninth. Again, vague suspicions curled in his mind. Two collisions between the same two men, even two years apart, might be coincidence, of course. But no matter what Kirkpatrick had said, a two-out bunt for a hit made sense only if it were unexpected, and Fleming's had not been.

McGreevy was also aware that Conroy could have made the easy move of throwing to first instead of waiting for the runner to reach him.

But Conroy was the man who was racked up two years ago, he mused. Why should Dixie be gunning for him? It ought to be the other way around.

"Hey, what do you know?"

The last remark was made aloud as Dave Alten followed Slade with another single, and activity started up in the Hornet bullpen. The Eagles still trailed by six, 9–3.

When Pete came out of the shower, he found both Adams and clubhouse man Marty Hull listening with rapt attention to the table radio in the middle of the room.

"What's going on, Case?"

"We got three runs in, two on and one out," Adams explained gleefully. "They're bringing in

145

another pitcher now. Charlie Temple's the hitter."

"How'd we do it?"

"Couple of hits, two walks, and an error. The guy in center misjudged a drive by Grey and then made a bum throw."

"Fleming?" Pete exclaimed. It was almost beyond belief.

"Naw, he's out of there. Clampett."

So Dixie had been enough shaken up to retire too, Pete thought.

The radio voice resumed. "We've got a pinch hitter as the first man to face Lindy Tippett, the Hornets' third pitcher in this ninth inning. It's Charlie Temple batting for the pitcher, Pete Conroy."

Adams grinned at Pete. "Wish you were up there swinging?"

Pete said he thought Temple might scare them a bit more. The trainer clucked at him not to stand there with only a towel around him. Temple smashed a double to right to drive in two more runs, and Pete was almost fully dressed before the inning ended with the Eagles scoring three more to take a 11–9 lead.

All three listened in fascination as Sil De Anza came on to get rid of the Hornets in the ninth. Then the Eagles, laughing and whooping happily, surged into the locker room, acting ten feet tall, as befitted a team that had scored eight times in the final inning to win a game counted as lost.

Freddie Villa came up and shook Pete's hand. "Hey, winning pitcher Conroy, nice work!"

Pete looked at him blankly.

"You get credit for the win," Villa barked. "Don't tell me you hadn't marked that down already."

"Honest, I hadn't even thought of it," Pete answered with such sincerity that the second baseman had to believe it.

"Crazy," he chirped as Meredith approached.

"Congratulations, Pete. I still think you made the wrong play on Dixie, but it won the ball game for us. Clampett blew a drive by Grey and then threw it where nobody could have caught it. I think Fleming would have had it easy. Anyway, that beat 'em."

"Is he hurt?" Pete asked.

"I dunno, except he had to sit out the ninth. That's not my worry."

Nor mine, Pete thought, but with some uneasiness.

Ace Elwood was next to stop in front of Pete's cubicle. "Good job, Pete," he said heartily. "Lots of mustard and good control, except the ball Dixie bunted. I told you to keep it high, remember?"

"Yeah, I sure was off on that one," Pete said, and Elwood gave him a quizzical stare before walking away.

In the midst of the cheerful hubbub, the Eagles went about the business of getting dressed with some alacrity, since their bus would be driven directly to the airport. The series with the Bengals would begin the next night.

Floyd McGreevy, looking even more rumpled

than usual, came into the room and sought out Meredith.

"Where's Conroy, Buzz?"

Meredith pointed, then asked, "Have you any word on Dixie?"

"I stopped by their dressing room, for a moment, but I didn't get much," McGreevy said. "Everyone was pretty low after blowing this game. Fleming was still in the treatment room, and all I could find out is that he hurt his shoulder. They're going to send him to the hospital for X rays. If anything's busted, he could be through for the season."

"I wouldn't like that," Meredith said somberly. "He's a fine ballplayer, for all his grandstanding. Did you talk to Kearns, Floyd?"

"He wasn't seeing any reporters right away. Can't blame him."

McGreevy sauntered over to Pete's locker. "Quite a coincidence, you and Fleming running into each other again," he began casually.

"You could call it that, I suppose," Pete said.

"It certainly wasn't your fault this time," the writer said. Pete, despite his wariness, fell into the trap.

"It wasn't my fault the first time," he retorted vehemently.

"Oh, you thought Fleming was to blame?" McGreevy was only mildly curious, it appeared.

"Honestly, I'd rather not talk about it." Pete wished he had kept his mouth shut. "It's all over and done with."

148

"Sure thing," McGreevy said in hearty agreement. "Anyway, nice pitching, Conroy."

All over and done with, my eye, Pete thought as McGreevy left.

"Shake it up, men, we've got a plane to catch," Meredith called. A few of the players had already left to board the bus. Pete picked up the suitcase with his personal effects as the clubhouse door swung open and Stu Berry entered in a rush, a look of concern on his face. He stopped as he caught sight of Pete.

"Hold it a minute," he said hurriedly. "Ah want to talk to you."

His eyes swept the room and he darted toward Meredith, leaving Pete puzzled and a little irritated. What could Berry want to discuss that wouldn't hold until they were on the bus?

The southpaw was talking volubly, but close to Meredith and in a voice low enough so that only the manager could hear.

"Ah think they're sorta waitin' on Conroy outside," he said breathlessly. "Sound mean, too. When Sil and I come out, they started yellin' at us, like 'Which one is Conroy? He better not come back here no more,' and stuff like that. Lucky me and Sil is too big to be mistook for Pete."

Meredith stared in disbelief. "Aren't there any police out there?" he demanded.

"Two or three, maybe. But you get someone started a-shovin' and a-yellin' and you got trouble if they spot Pete."

"Blasted idiots!" Meredith spat the words, but

149

there was a look of apprehension in his eyes. "We still have to put our equipment on that bus. I suppose if we moved it to another exit, they'd just follow it. Is Pete still here?"

"Yeah, I stopped him and asked him to wait. There he is."

"Good boy. You think there'd be any trouble if the rest of us went out together?"

"Ah don't think so, Buzz; Sil got through all right. They's looking for a little fella."

"Tell Pete I want to talk to him. Hey, Ace."

He beckoned to Elwood. Pete waited for Berry with growing impatience and was bewildered when the pitcher said, "See you on the bus, Pete. Right now, Buzz wants you."

"What is this?" Pete asked crossly, but moved toward the manager, who was talking earnestly to Elwood. The catcher's features mirrored sheer amazement.

"Pete, I want you to go with Ace right to the airport. Leave your bag here; we'll take it on the bus. See you on the plane."

"What? Why?" Pete could only sputter.

"Never mind the questions now," Meredith said savagely. "You follow Ace and I'll tell you later. Give me your bag."

He practically wrenched the suitcase out of Pete's grasp and gave him a slight shove. Elwood, looking suddenly grim and determined, said quietly, "Let's go, Pete."

He started for the door, the dumbfounded Pete at his heels. Outside, Ace turned left toward

150

the regular exit, but halfway down the corridor, swung right into another passageway.

"Hey, that goes back into the stadium," Pete protested.

"I know. Stay close to me."

He walked swiftly, Pete hurrying to keep up. They emerged in the lower grandstand, now empty except for men picking up discarded seat cushions and sweeping the littered runways. They followed the curve of the stands for perhaps 50 feet before the catcher turned left again into another passageway marked EXIT. In a moment they were underneath the stadium structure and passing through one of the gates that fans used.

Out on the sidewalk Elwood paused, looked up and down the street, then motioned to a taxi at the head of the waiting row.

"Get in," he told Pete. "The airport, driver."

Once under way, Elwood exhaled noisily and wiped his forehead with a handkerchief.

"Maybe," Pete said with elaborate indifference, "you can tell me why we came out like a couple of fugitives."

"Yeah, maybe I can," the catcher said. And he did. Pete found it hard to believe at first, but when he saw that Elwood was absolutely in earnest, he was shaken.

"You really think there might have been trouble?"

"Buzz thought so after he heard Stu. Why take chances?"

"But how can they blame me when it was Dixie

151

who knocked me over? That doesn't make sense," Pete complained.

"There's nothing rational about a mob," Elwood said, and fixed Pete with a steady gaze.

"It's none of my business if you and Fleming have a thing going, but I'll tell you frankly I think you went out of your way looking for action. First, you give him a perfect pitch to bunt and then you wait for him when a throw gets him by 20 feet. I admit it looked as if he was going for you, and he got the worst of it. But I won't buy any yarn that it just happened."

Pete's blue eyes clouded and he did not reply at once. "All right, Ace, we do have a thing," he said in a low voice. "Anyway, I'll admit I had one with him. I didn't realize it went both ways until today, when he tried to get me on the base line. And I don't know why. Not because I tried to deck him, I'm certain. The ball wasn't near his head."

"No, it wasn't. Inside, but not much, and around his shoulders."

Pete felt the old bitterness rising in him once more. "And what right has he to be sore?" he asked angrily. "He wasn't hurt two years ago; I was, and it cost me my job."

"It was an accident, though, wasn't it?" Ace inquired, frowning. "You don't think he deliberately ran you down?"

"No, not deliberately." Pete's voice quivered with wrath. "Just stupidly, because of the grandstanding hot dog he is and always will be. He had the gall to say it was really my own fault. He didn't even seem sorry about it!"

"How did the play go, exactly?" Elwood asked persuasively. Pete had no difficulty recalling it.

"Well, the center fielder does call the shots when more than one man has a chance for the ball," the catcher pointed out. "He has the best view of the field."

"Of course! But he didn't call me off — as a matter of fact, I signaled I had it and I heard Tex White yell that it was mine. Dixie didn't pay any attention; he was too busy trying to show what a great outfielder he was."

Elwood nodded in sympathy. "Maybe he did you a favor, Pete," he said lightly. "You might turn out to be a better pitcher than you were anything else. Forget about Dixie and get the ball over."

Pete laughed without mirth as the taxi entered the brightly lighted road to the airport terminal.

"Much obliged, Ace. And I'd appreciate it if you didn't mention to anyone else what I've told you — how I feel about Fleming."

It was the catcher's turn to laugh. "I promise. But if you think that's an official secret after what happened today, you're not as bright as you look."

It was as Ace predicted.

The taxi had beaten the slower bus to the airport by ten minutes, but when the Eagles streamed into the terminal, they were talking about little else.

That included Floyd McGreevy, who had left with the players, had run the gauntlet of noisy and unruly hecklers outside the stadium, and heard the

153

loud voices, threatening, seeking to identify Pete Conroy.

He had also discovered that Conroy was not on the team bus and promptly sought out Meredith to ask if Pete had missed it.

"No, he didn't miss it," the manager said brusquely, and explained the circumstances.

"You'll be doing everyone a favor, Mac, if you soft-pedal that part. I don't want any buildup of a feud between Conroy and Fleming."

"From what I saw, it doesn't need any buildup," the writer said aggrievedly. "What if Dixie is out for the season and the Hornets make a big flap about it? I can't pretend to my boss that I didn't know anything about it. Be reasonable, Buzz."

Meredith looked harassed, but he understood. "O.K., I leave it to your judgment, Floyd."

McGreevy gave a disgusted snort, but knew that he would hold off until the extent of Fleming's injury was determined.

Richie Shipstein eased into the seat next to Pete as the plane took off.

"Please accept my sincere congratulations," he began with exaggerated formality, "for choosing friend Dixie. I was hoping you'd stick it in his ear, though."

"I didn't choose him, he chose me," Pete protested.

"Congratulations, anyway. I wish he'd broken his neck."

CHAPTER 12

THE EAGLES learned next day that Dixie hadn't broken anything. He had a bruised shoulder that would keep him on the bench for a day or two longer, that was all. In the news stories carried by the wire services, there was no indication that his colliding with the pitcher was anything more than the kind of mishap that occurred as part of the game.

Pete was truly relieved. Regardless of his feelings toward The Actor, he did not want to be singled out as the man who had deliberately put him out of commission, particularly since that was not true.

The Eagles broke even in four games with the Bengals. They might have won three but for two errors by Bobby Britton at shortstop. Leo Brown was in the throes of a batting slump, and Don Snyder, the other reserve infielder, was a notoriously light hitter. The Eagles felt the loss of shortstop Andy Emmerick more than that of the two pitchers hurt in the same accident.

Their pitching against the Bengals was uniformly excellent, even though they lost two games. But it was a different story on the next stop against the

Generals. Mike North was knocked out early in the opener, and neither De Anza nor Dolin could shut off the trickle of runs thereafter.

In the second game of the set, Shipstein got into difficulties because Villa kicked one and then Dave Alten dropped a throw. But Ben Wakeley, the Eagles' left fielder, put them back in business with a three-run homer and it was only 5–4 in the Generals' favor when they batted in the bottom of the seventh.

Berry and Smith, who had warmed up intermittently for three innings, started again, and after a call from the bench, Varnell pointed at Pete.

"You too, Conroy."

Pete rose with alacrity. Because of the efficiency of the starting pitchers against the Bengals, he had been sitting down to the point of restlessness.

Shipstein went to three balls and no strikes on the first hitter and Berry began to throw harder. Moments later, the left-hander was waved to duty, with two men on base and one out.

Berry disposed of the next batter on a pop fly, but then walked his successor on four straight pitches to load them up. Meredith came out in a slow stroll, talked briefly with Berry and Elwood, then signaled to the bullpen.

"You're up, Pete," Varnell said laconically and walked to the gate with him. He knew the situation, knew the hitter, and knew why Meredith had summoned Pete instead of the more experienced Smith. But he made no comment. Pitching instructions would come from the manager, not from the coach.

The batter was Rusty Stark, a right-handed swinger.

"Move the ball around on this guy," Meredith advised. "But whatever you do, don't walk him."

Pete warmed up from the full windup. After his final preliminary pitch, Elwood came out to the mound again.

"He'll be looking at the first one. Just get it over."

Pete got it over, the sidearm fast ball, and Stark looked. He looked at the second one too, which was wide and in the dirt. Pete's heart leaped with apprehension as Elwood fell to his knees, but the backstop blocked it and smothered it with his mitt.

Pete discovered that he was jumpy. He had come in so intent on retiring the one batter that he had not had time before to get nervous.

Don't walk him; get it over, he repeated to himself.

Elwood asked for the fast ball, outside and low. Pete coiled and threw. It was the fast ball, no doubt of it, but it was waist high and it broke only slightly. Stark fell on it with a fearful smash and Pete knew at once that the ball was going a long way.

He whirled and saw Phil Slade, in center field, turn his back to the diamond and take off in the direction of the fence. He had not played very deep because Stark was not noted as a long-ball hitter. Just as he reached the warning path, the ten-foot wide strip of dirt that informed the fielder of the fence's proximity, Slade jumped and reached high

157

to grab the high drive under the sign that marked the distance to home plate — 410 feet.

The fans' joyful shouts of anticipation as the ball arched toward center field shut off abruptly at Slade's catch. Pete walked to the bench, somewhat shaken. As Slade loped in, he said, "Great play, Phil. I didn't think you had a chance."

"Oh, I only wanted to make it look hard," the center fielder said lightly, to conceal his obvious satisfaction. "I didn't think the little devil could hit one that far."

"All right, let's get some runs," Meredith said impatiently. "Conroy, what were you doing? That last pitch looked like it didn't have a thing on it. It was a batting practice pitch right in the fat part."

"I got it up too high," Pete said contritely. "It didn't break much."

"Well, don't get careless again," the manager admonished and advanced to his customary observation point at the top of the dugout steps. Pete looked at the batting order posted on the dugout wall and saw that the pitcher would hit second. He went over to the bat rack and was examining the assorted lumber when Freddie Villa hit a bad hop grounder that the third baseman could not handle.

Meredith looked over his shoulder and said, "Jarvis. Get up there. Watch for the hit-and-run."

Wendell Jarvis, the Eagles' fourth outfielder, reached for his batting helmet, and Pete turned away from the rack in sudden disappointment. He had been eager to swing a bat for the first time in
158

an Eagle uniform, and privately he considered himself a pretty good hand at hitting behind the runner.

Still, it was logical to pinch hit for the pitcher in these circumstances and he slid into a seat near the end of the bench. Jarvis went out to the first baseman, but Villa made second and scored with the tying run, as Jim Grey whistled a single over third base.

The Eagles' bench greeted Villa happily, then Grey and Ben Wakeley exuberantly as the burly outfielder belted his second home run of the day for a 7–5 lead. Meredith, beaming, caught sight of Pete as he was among the welcoming committee to greet the grinning Wakeley, and ordered him to the showers. Pete departed reluctantly. He would have liked to watch the finish from the bench.

Shipstein, who had gone in earlier in the inning, and Berry, who had followed him, were still in uniform, the radio blaring loudly. Duane Smith had come in to pitch the eighth.

"Hiya, Petey," Berry greeted him gaily. "That was a real long out you got Stark to hit, but it was a out and that's what counts. I'll take 'em like that every time."

"I'd rather not, Rebel," Pete said ruefully. "I got two years older waiting for the ball to come down."

Shipstein, a towel draped around his neck, rumbled something unintelligible. He was obviously disgusted.

"You better root some, Petey," Berry advised. "This is your game to win, you know. Duane can lose it, but he can't win it unless they tie it up first."

Once again it had failed to register on Pete that because he had been the pitcher of record when the Eagles went ahead in the top of the eighth, he would be credited with the victory, if it was a victory. And he could not be charged with the loss if the Generals rallied to pull it out.

Winning pitcher — Conroy, he thought. It would look nice in the box score. But it was only a freak result of the established rules for baseball scoring. He had pitched to one man and thrown him what would have been a triple save for Slade's skill. So the victory was Pete's, and Shipstein, who had pitched seven innings of creditable ball only to be betrayed by errors, got nothing. Small wonder Richie appeared disgruntled.

Smith yielded nothing in the eighth, a run in the ninth, and Dan Dolin came on to retire the last man to assure Pete of his second win as a major-league pitcher.

Which I am not — yet, he admitted frankly to himself. On the other hand, it had not been proved that he wasn't one.

This point was under discussion between Meredith and Jim Varnell.

"He gives me the whim-whams," the manager said. "I can still hear the noise of Stark's hit. But we won the game. What do you do about that?"

"He may be one of the lucky ones," Varnell said. "That's as good as having six different pitches."

"He can't be that lucky every time. You should've seen what he threw Stark. A flat curve, up here. If his pitch doesn't break down, it's no good. The batter can follow it all the way, like Stark did."

Varnell said he thought Pete's delivery should be altered slightly from the full sidearm to more nearly three quarters. He imitated the motion.

"He's throwing from here," he demonstrated, "when he ought to be up here."

"All right, have him try it, Jim."

Pete accepted the suggestion without protest, although the slight variation in his delivery affected his control at first. He had to adjust his leg motion too, and when he pitched batting practice or in the bullpen, he threw a lot of balls into the dirt. Both Varnell and Ace Elwood offered reassurance.

"Better to be wild low than wild high," the catcher said. "The league is full of high ball hitters."

He did not pitch again on the balance of the road trip, but he did play. In the seventh inning of a game with the Chicks, Leo Brown was scraped on the hand making a tag at second base. The wound was superficial, but needed attention, and as Meredith and trainer Adams examined it, the manager had a sudden thought. The Eagles were trailing, 6–1; neither Bobby Britton nor Don Snyder had been playing particularly well, and Meredith remembered that he had an infielder in the bullpen.

Duane Smith was the only pitcher active in that area when the phone rang. Pete was astonished when it rang and Varnell said, "You're wanted, Conroy."

He jumped up and started to unbutton his jacket, eager to get warmed up.

"Not to pitch, Pete," the coach said with a faint smile. "They want you now — to play short-stop."

"Shortstop?" Pete said the word as though he had never heard it before.

"That's what the man said. Better hustle."

Somewhat confused, Pete nearly tripped getting through the gate, but he reached Meredith in a hurry.

"I guess I don't have to tell you anything about this job," the manager said. "Temple will position you, and you can talk to Freddie."

"I think I can remember," Pete said.

"Hey, they're bringing in a pitcher to play short," said a Chicks writer in the press box. "Sort of unusual, isn't it?"

"No more so than bringing in a shortstop to pitch," Floyd McGreevy said, chuckling. "We've already done that, and besides, this guy wasn't a bad infielder — with the Hornets a couple of years ago."

"Oh, it's *that* Conroy."

Unlike his approach as a reliever, Pete was not at all nervous as he stationed himself at short.

After all, he was only a few weeks away from a regular infield job.

With one out and the bases empty, the infield played in normal depth, shaded slightly toward second base for the left-handed hitter facing Bill Kosecki. The Chick topped a sinking fast ball and dribbled it slowly toward short, out of the pitcher's reach.

Pete charged the ball, scooped, and threw underhand while still on the move. Alten had to stretch for the throw, but it was there on time.

Villa yelled approval at Pete, who was pleased with himself.

Just as long as they hit 'em in front of me, he thought.

Pete had one more chance that day, going almost to the stands to chase a high foul back of third on which Grey, the third baseman, and Wakely, the left fielder, also were converging. As he moved under the ball, he experienced a flash of panic. He thought he could hear the sound of Wakeley's spikes behind him. But they did not come near and Pete made the catch, his unreasoning fear receding as swiftly as it had appeared.

He knew, however, that this was only a late inning experiment by Meredith, not likely to be repeated. He was a pitcher.

The Eagles were in fourth place when they returned home to meet the Robins, Capitols, Gold Sox, and Hornets. The Hornets were in first place, but only three games in front of the Eagles. It was still anybody's race.

The Robins were a miserable last and played like it for two games, then became pesty in the third and final contest. Mike North, with a 6–2 lead going into the ninth, gave up two runs in a hurry, and there were runners on first and third with two away when Meredith decided that was enough for North.

Next up for the Robins was their leading hitter, Cardenal, a right-hander, and Meredith was certain he would not be replaced, since he could hit right-handers as well as southpaws. A low-breaking pitch was the best weapon against him, and if Conroy had anything, that was it. Besides, Berry and De Anza were also warmed up if Conroy did not get Cardenal. Even a long out would end the game. Meredith decided to gamble.

"Keep it down and don't give him anything he can pull," was all he told the expectant Pete.

Pete moved Cardenal back with his first delivery, making him spin away from an inside fast ball, not a beanball, but due warning to the hitter that he would crowd the plate at his own risk.

He missed outside with the modified cross fire, not feeling entirely natural with the three-quarter delivery. But the next one was on the corner at the knees and Cardenal went for it. He topped it, rolling a grounder that Villa gobbled easily for the game-ending out.

"Attaboy, Pete," Jim Grey called as he ran past Pete toward the dugout, and Meredith came out to give him a quick handshake and a pat on the back. Pete had the feeling that he had made the team and no longer faced the possibility of being sent down to New Bristol.

He could not know that the day before, Buzz Meredith had suggested exactly that move to Paul Gordon, the club vice-president, who had rejected it.

"I have to admit that Paul has a point," the manager told Jim Varnell thoughtfully. "They haven't scored on Conroy yet. But he's green and he needs work, steady work. He could pitch every fourth day at New Bristol and he can't do that here. Gordon said Pete had already won two games for us, which is true, but he's forgotten how he won 'em. They knocked the stitches off the ball, but somebody caught it, and we went out and got a flock of runs. I don't call that pitching."

The talk with the vice-president was still in Meredith's mind when he summoned Pete to face Cardenal. There was no fault to find with that effort, the manager conceded. He also admitted to himself that part of his reluctance stemmed from the manner in which Conroy had been thrust upon him from the top.

Pete pitched an inning and one third three days later against the Capitols, walking one and giving up a single, but no runs. He did not work against the Gold Sox, to his disappointment. He and Meredith were in agreement on one thing — he needed work.

The Hornets came in for a four-game series, now

only one game in front of the Eagles. Fred Kearns, arms folded across his ample chest, leaned on the back of the batting cage watching his players take batting practice before the opener. Meredith strolled over to join him.

"How's Dixie, Fred?" he asked casually. Kearns eyed him questioningly.

"He's all right, Buzz. Are you figuring on pitching Conroy in this series?"

"I might. Why?"

"I don't know. Dixie hasn't said anything since he got hurt and that's what bothers me. Usually, if he thinks somebody's been throwing at him, or trying to get tough, he spouts off plenty about what he's going to do to the guy next time. I don't mean fighting; he's never been trouble that way. But bearing down extra hard. I know he's sore at Conroy, but he hasn't mentioned his name that I know of since that run-in."

"Funny he should be the one who's sore," Meredith said. "After all, he's the one who put Pete out of commission to start with. Whose fault was it, Fred?"

"It wasn't anyone's fault," Kearns said testily. "Just one of those things, that's all."

"Well, if Fleming thinks he was to blame, maybe this is his way of showing it. You know how it is — borrow money from a man or do him an injury and you get to dislike him because you feel under obligation to him. I've seen a few friendships go up that spout."

166

"Quite the homely philosopher, aren't you?" Kearns said with something like a sneer.

Meredith bristled. "I don't think Conroy was throwing at him, and I think Dixie was asking for trouble on that bunt," he said doggedly. "But I do know we thought it smart to sneak Pete out the back way because some of your fans were acting up pretty mean. You heard about that?"

"I heard about it," Kearns acknowledged gruffly. "I don't think anything would have happened, though."

"Maybe not. Let's keep it that way."

Pete and Dixie Fleming did not pass within 20 feet of each other before the game, nor did their paths cross during it. Richie Shipstein pitched a four-hit, 3–0 shutout, getting Fleming four times.

The pitcher seemed happier about that than he did about the victory itself. "You notice I dusted him twice," he said exultantly, "but he didn't do that swan dive. That's the act he saves for the yokels at home."

Jack Gregg was not so fortunate the next day. He had a 1–0 lead going into the eighth, then seemed to lose his stuff all at once. The Hornets had three runs in and men on first and second before either De Anza or Pete could loosen up.

Fleming was approaching the batter's box as Meredith disconsolately signaled for time and went to the mound, still undecided on which of his relievers to bring in. He knew that De Anza, though his most reliable relief pitcher, had not been too successful against Dixie. Conroy was still an un-

167

known quantity, but Meredith had the feeling that he would undoubtedly put out an extra effort against this man. Just one out was all the manager wanted from him; De Anza could pitch the ninth.

So it was Pete who emerged through the bullpen gate and as he neared the diamond, Ken Kirkpatrick, the Hornet writer, exclaimed, "Hey, isn't that Conroy?"

"Yep," said Floyd McGreevy. He speculated on the possibility of more fireworks between the two.

Much the same thoughts were running through Pete Conroy's mind as he handed his jacket to the bat boy, took the ball from Jack Gregg, and saw who was standing by the batter's box.

Meredith studied Pete closely. "This guy bother you particularly?"

"He's just another fellow with a bat. I'll try to get him out, that's all."

"That's the idea. He may expect to be brushed back, but don't throw high. Jam him tight, then low and away."

"I don't think he'll be bunting," Ace Elwood said jokingly.

Neither do I, Pete thought. He didn't win anything last time.

CHAPTER 13

FLEMING LEANED CASUALLY against his bat as Pete warmed up from the stretch position from which he would have to pitch. He seemed uninterested in what Pete was throwing.

But when Pete was ready to pitch, Dixie was not ready to bat. He asked for time to get something out of his eye. Pete viewed the maneuver with scorn. It was a bush league device aimed at making the pitcher fret over a delay.

Dixie stepped in at last and Pete whizzed the fast ball, belt-high, on the inside. Fleming let it go, making a slight arc of his body. Pete thought it could have been a strike, but the umpire did not.

He threw a good strike on the outside and Dixie let it go. Elwood signaled for the fork ball, the change of pace. With a seemingly effortless swing, Fleming hit it on a line over Villa's head between right and center field.

Pete whirled to see the ball rolling to the fence with Phil Slade and Johnny Key in frantic pursuit. It was a certain double, probably a triple, he thought in misery, and automatically moved to a position behind third base as Jim Grey set himself to take the relay.

The two runners scored easily. Fleming, following the sign from Corky Schmidt that a slide was unnecessary, came to third standing up. Pete took the ball from Grey and walked back to the mound, calling himself names.

Meredith, poised on the dugout steps, was on the verge of calling in De Anza, but while he was hesitating, Pete was preparing to pitch to Willie Gaines. The damage was done, anyway, the manager thought gloomily. The Eagles now trailed by 5–1, and that was a good deal harder to overcome than 3–1.

Elwood pointed toward third base, a warning to Pete to see that Fleming did not get too big a lead, and perhaps try to steal home. That would be the final humiliation, Pete thought, and came off the rubber to bluff a throw that sent Dixie back.

Low and away was the sign for Gaines, and Pete unwound. It was far too low and too much away, a pitch that hit in front of the plate and skidded under Elwood's mitt to the base of the grandstand.

Pete knew it was a bad effort as soon as it left his hand. He was down from the mound and racing for the plate as Gaines, backing out of the box, waved Fleming on in.

Elwood scrambled after the ball, retrieved it, and fired to Pete a low throw on his gloved hand side that would have made it easy to Pete to make a sweeping tag on the sliding runner.

But Fleming did not slide. He had the throw beaten under any circumstances, and he chose to come in standing up a split second before the ball reached Pete, who was waiting at the plate with his back to Fleming. He had no chance to get out of Fleming's way.

So Pete went one way, the ball another, and Pete's cap still a third as Dixie ran into him crossing the plate. Pete landed on his hands and knees, more startled than anything else.

When he realized what had happened, he jumped to his feet, his face livid. Dixie Fleming was trotting to the Hornets' bench and Pete's immediate impulse was to follow him.

But Ace Elwood had anticipated his move. He interposed his padded frame between the fuming pitcher and the visitors' dugout.

"Easy does it, lad," he said softly, but with firmness.

"Easy!" Pete exploded. "I'm not going to let that bum knock me around like a tenpin!"

"You all right, Pete?" It was Buzz Meredith's voice, and Pete spun around to face him, eyes blazing.

"Sure, I'm all right! All I want is a crack at that big hot dog!"

Willie Gaines, standing by the plate had been listening with undisguised interest.

"Petey, you was blocking the plate on him," he said with a sly grin. "He had to do somethin' to get past you."

"Look, Willie," Pete said through clenched

teeth, "you tell your friend he'd better stay loose next time, because I'm going to drill a hole through him!"

"Shut up, Conroy," Meredith's voice was tense with fury. "Go cool off in the clubhouse."

Meredith stepped up to the plate umpire to inform him that he was changing pitchers.

Willie Gaines, still grinning, said, "I'll deliver your message, Petey."

Shaking with rage but stunned by Meredith's abrupt command, Pete picked up his cap, brushed the dirt from it, and walked slowly to the dugout. He went down the steps and into the tunnel that led to the dressing room without so much as a glance at his teammates on the bench.

Shipstein, about to offer words of sympathy, looked surprised. "I'd say our buddy is a little red-necked," he commented to Mike North. "Was it the triple or the way Dixie flattened him?"

"Probably both. At that, Dixie could have slid in. He had the throw beaten anyway and he didn't have to run into Conroy. I somehow get the idea those two don't like each other."

"Really? What ever made you think that?" Shipstein asked in mock amazement.

The shower cooled Pete physically, but did nothing to dampen his inner turmoil. In his fury, he had forgotten for the moment that the triple and the wild pitch did not represent the ultimate in relief pitching. Not until he had come out of the shower room and seen the Eagles come tramping

172

into the clubhouse did his mind focus on his own lack of efficiency.

When he discovered that the Eagles had scored twice in the ninth to lose, 6–3, his spirits plummeted. If he had retired Fleming, the teams would still be playing. The defeat would be charged officially to Jack Gregg, but the man responsible for it was Pete Conroy.

Meredith, glowering, halted briefly by his side. "Come see me when you get dressed," he said brusquely.

Pete went into the manager's office braced for a going-over. He got it, but not along the lines he had expected.

"You didn't pitch too good, Conroy," Meredith began coldly, "but that's not what I want to talk about. Fellow like Fleming hits the best of us and a wild pitch — well, it was unfortunate."

He pointed a menacing finger at Pete.

"But when you threaten openly to skull a batter, you're making a mess of trouble for yourself, for me and everyone on this club. I'll give you the benefit of the doubt — I don't believe you meant it; you were just hot. But what you said went back to Fleming and to Fred Kearns and to the newspapers, that's certain."

Pete, his thin features taut and pale, avoided the manager's icy gaze. He kept his eyes fixed on a spot on the wall beyond Meredith's shoulder.

"Suppose you do hit somebody?" Meredith demanded. "Or Shipstein or Gregg or North let a pitch get away from them and plunk a batter.

That happens often enough by mistake. But on account of your big mouth, they could be accused of doing it on purpose, and I'll be in the grease, too, for telling them to do it.

"Every umpire in the league will be watching us like hawks on high-inside pitches and if one gets a little too close, blooey, our pitchers get a warning, and maybe tossed out. On account of your pop-off, Conroy, we have to be awful careful about brushing back a hitter. For a while, anyway."

Pete said sullenly that he wasn't the first pitcher ever to make threats. Furthermore, every pitcher moved the batter back to keep him from taking a toehold at the plate.

"Of course," Meredith said impatiently. "But do you think any of 'em actually want to hit a man in the head? I've seen a few beaned in my time, some of them badly hurt before they made everyone wear batting helmets. And nearly every time, it ruined the pitcher who did it. All he could see after that was the man he'd hit, lying on the ground.

"No, sir," Meredith continued emphatically, "no one does that. You see a man hit in the head, it's an accident. One more thing. You want to settle things with Fleming, do it off the field. Take a cutlass to him after the season if you want, but while you're on this team, lay off. That's all."

Pete turned without a word and was at the door when the manager called after him.

"One thing I almost forgot. For sounding off to

Gaines, you're fined 50 dollars. Next time it won't be so cheap."

The manager sat scowling at the door for a while after it had closed behind Pete. He had deliberately exaggerated the possible effects of Conroy's outburst for a dual purpose. One was to impress upon the pitcher the importance of keeping his lip buttoned. More immediate was Meredith's genuine concern that it might touch off a real vendetta between the Hornets and the Eagles, one that could extend beyond the Conroy-Fleming area. He had seen that happen before and nobody had won. It was quite possible that the Hornet pitchers, informed of Pete's threat, would come out tomorrow ready to knock down every batter. The Eagles would retaliate, of course, in self-protection. The prospect was not a pleasant one.

Pete was beginning to grow indignant by the time he left Meredith. He headed straight for the door, but the bulky figure of Floyd McGreevy cut him off.

"I hear you threatened to throw at Dixie Fleming the next chance you get," the sportswriter began. "Is that right?"

Pete stopped and made an effort to choose his words carefully. "I'm sorry, Mr. McGreevy. I don't want to say anything now. I'm late for a date already."

He stepped around the writer and hurried out. He did not have a date and he did not know exactly where he was headed, but he certainly did not want to be interviewed.

Irritated, McGreevy sought out Elwood and asked the same question. The catcher, somewhat apologetic, advised him that he had better get the details from the manager.

Meredith was not disposed to be communicative at first.

"Conroy was sore and shot off his face," he said with assumed indifference. "He didn't mean anything by it."

"Oh, he didn't?" McGreevy said with sarcasm. "Go across the hall and tell that to Fred Kearns. He's steaming. You've got a real headhunters' contest in the oven, Buzz."

Meredith's eyebrows came together. "Did Fleming explain why he knocked Conroy down instead of hooking around him?" he demanded challengingly.

"He was real sweet about it. He saw the plate was blocked and he had to get to it and if Conroy was going to throw at him, he'd just have to risk it and hope he'd hit another triple. Very cute fella, that Dixie."

Meredith growled in his throat.

"But Kearns had smoke coming out of his ears," McGreevy continued. "So did some of the others, and the writers know it. It's perfectly plain these two are gunning for each other."

"Who's gunning for who?" Meredith asked, suddenly angry. "Fleming busted up Conroy when they were on the Hornets and twice now he's run into him when he didn't have to. What's Conroy done to him, tell me that!"

"Well, he did say he was going to drill him. Are you going to use him against the Hornets again, Buzz?"

"I don't know. That's all I'll say now, Floyd. Sorry."

McGreevy departed huffily. At the moment, Meredith had no intention of pitching Pete Conroy against the Hornets, no matter what the relief needs might be. And not because Fleming had hit him for a triple, either. There had been nothing wrong with the pitch; Ace Elwood had confirmed that.

"It was a low change-up, the fork ball, and Dixie just nailed it," the catcher said regretfully. "He didn't hit it squarely, but you know the kind of power he has."

"Yeah," Meredith said moodily. "I know."

As for Pete, he went downtown and had dinner alone, hardly aware of what he was eating. He realized he had been stupid to yell about what he was going to do next time he faced The Actor. He hoped fervently that the newspapers didn't make too much of it.

The newspapers did what they could. There were quotes from Fred Kearns: "If the Eagles want trouble, they can have it," a bland denial by Dixie Fleming that he held any hard feelings toward Conroy, "unless he has a grudge against me for that accident two years ago," and pointed reference to the silence on the part of Pete and Meredith. Silence, it was obviously implied, went a long way toward confirming the truth of the charges.

Somewhat chastened by the uproar he had created, Pete slipped unobtrusively into the dressing room before the next night's game. From now on, he vowed, he would concentrate on playing baseball, not talking about it.

But as he ran around the outfield, he had not put Fleming out of his thoughts entirely. Dixie would remain unfinished business in Pete's private file.

He reported to the bullpen as usual, to be greeted by Stu Berry.

"Ah nevah picked you for no fire eater, Petey. Will you really stick one in his ear next time?"

"No comment," Pete said sourly, and even Varnell smiled. He knew about the 50-dollar fine.

It was a humid, late-summer night with no hint of a breeze. The crowd was noisy and restless as Bill Kosecki of the Eagles and Grady Jones of the visitors hooked up in a fine mound duel. If the Hornets won it, they would tie for first place. There was tension in the air, particularly in the light of the previous day's incident.

But no batter was knocked down. Both pitchers were sharp. The Hornets scored one in the second inning; Dave Alten tied it with a long homer in the fifth; the Hornets took a 2–1 lead in the sixth.

In that inning, Jim Grey suffered a slight muscle pull while sliding into second, and Bobby Britton replaced him at third base.

Jones encountered his first real difficulty in the

178

seventh. He filled the bases with two out, with Leo Brown scheduled to bat next. But Brown had struck out twice swinging against Jones, and it was getting late in the game. Meredith sent Charlie Temple up to hit for Brown and had Don Snyder, his remaining infielder, warm up to replace Leo at shortstop.

Temple hit the ball solidly, but not far enough The left fielder gathered it in and the score stayed at 2–1.

It was still 2–1 when the Eagles came to bat in the bottom of the ninth and the crowd began to stomp in rhythm, demanding action. It was rewarded at once by Ben Wakely, who beat out a high chopper down the third-base line.

One run behind and playing at home, the Eagles went for the tying run. Johnny Key bunted Wakely to second, bringing up Freddie Villa, with Snyder and Kosecki, the pitcher, to follow, if the inning went that far.

Meredith went to the phone. "Get Berry up," he ordered Varnell. "And send Yerkes and Conroy in pronto."

Pete and the catcher came out of the gate on the run, passing Temple on the way to the bullpen to help out with warm-ups. Pete figured that Yerkes was going to hit for somebody, but he was puzzled about what was in store for him.

He realized what it was when he saw Jarvis kneeling in the on-deck circle, ready to follow Villa and bat for Snyder. The Eagles were out of infielders.

Villa hit a slow grounder to the right side of the infield to push Wakely to third while Freddie was being thrown out.

Jarvis walked to the plate as Yerkes figured the bat rack. If Jarvis went out, it was all over. If he were safe, and Wakely scored, Kosecki would bat for himself and continue to pitch. But if Jarvis drew a walk, then Yerkes would bat for Kosecki for the chance to tie it up.

Fred Kearns came out of the dugout to talk to Jones at this juncture. Jarvis was a more dangerous hitter than Yerkes (Kearns knew to the man what Eagle pinch hitters were still available) and the manager preferred to take his chances with Yerkes rather than give Jarvis anything good to swing at.

"Pitch to him, but don't give him anything fat," he instructed the pitcher.

Meredith, who also knew what Kearns had in mind, ordered Jarvis to lay off the first offering. It was outside by a foot. Jones tempted the hitter with two more pitches that were just a little off the plate, then walked him.

"All right, Tad, we can use one," the manager said as Yerkes went out to swing for Kosecki.

Grady hummed one on Yerkes' fists, an inside strike if it went by. The catcher chopped at it, sending a spinning grounder between first and second. The first baseman lunged desperately for it and missed; the second baseman, coming from the other direction and ten feet behind him, stretched for it too. It went under his glove and into right field as Wakely scored, and the crowd stormed approval. ˙

Jones put his hands on his hips and stood on the mound in an attitude of frustration and disgust. Yerkes grinned at him from first and Jarvis perched on second.

"That ball had eyes," Dave Alten drawled. It did seem as though the sphere had changed directions to avoid the gloves.

Britton, replacing Jim Grey as leadoff, had a chance to end the game, but could only fly out to right. Duane Smith, who had been working in the bullpen since the eighth inning, came in to pitch the tenth as Pete ran out to shortstop.

Smith got rid of the first Hornet, but Tex White belted one into left field. When Wakely had trouble picking up the ball, White, making the wide turn at first, continued to run. Pete, straddling the bag, took Wakely's throw too late to make the tag.

As Tex rose and brushed himself off, he remarked, "Hey, you better cool off on Dixie, Pete. He doesn't get mad easy, but I wouldn't throw at him like you said. Could be trouble."

"Tell him to quit running into me, then," Pete retorted angrily. "You were there the first time he did it, Tex."

"Yeah, I was there," the Hornet acknowledged in an odd tone.

White did not score. Neither did the Eagles, and Dixie Fleming was the first man to face Smith in the eleventh. He went to three-and-two on Fleming, then missed with a curve outside, and Dixie walked to first.

With Willie Gaines, a right-handed batter, at the plate, Villa would cover the bag on an attempted steal and Pete was secretly relieved. He wished to avoid any possible close quarters contact with Dixie at the moment, in view of Meredith's warning.

Dixie came down on the one-and-one pitch, getting a good jump on Smith's delivery. Elwood had no chance and Fleming was safe by feet.

Pete moved a step to his right for Gaines, leaving Villa the task of keeping Fleming close to the bag by feinting to sneak behind him. Dixie could have been ten miles away for all the notice Pete took of him.

Smith threw Gaines a curve and Willie hit a grass cutter under the pitcher's glove. Fleming broke for third without hesitation as Pete went to his left. He scooped the ball with one hand as Villa shrieked, "Third base, Pete, third!"

Pete knew he had Gaines if he threw to first, but in an extra inning, no-out situation, the leading runner was the important one. He whirled and snapped the ball toward Britton at third.

Britton reached to his gloved hand side for the throw, which was a foot off the ground. Whether it would have beaten Dixie, Pete never knew. The Hornet launched into a slide ten feet from the bag, involuntarily throwing up his arms as he went in. The ball struck him just above the right elbow and rolled a few feet into left field. Britton retrieved it quickly and his bluff throw held Gaines at first.

Pete stood frozen as he saw Fleming roll around, clutching his right arm. Fred Kearns lumbered out of the dugout to join Corky Schmidt, the coach, and helped Fleming to his feet.

Dixie was grimacing as he flexed his arm. The Hornets' trainer gently explored the sore portion, and Fleming winced again. Reluctantly he permitted himself to be led to the bench and a pinch runner took his place at third.

Pete, looking unhappy, approached Smith. "Sorry, Duane," he offered glumly. "I thought I had him."

"Not your fault," the reliever said curtly, as Meredith and Britton came to the mound.

"What do I have to do to keep you and Dixie apart?" the manager demanded in exasperation. "Hide you under a bed?"

"Do you think I tried to hit him?" Pete exclaimed hotly. "I want to win the ball game!"

Meredith seemed slightly taken aback.

"It was a good throw, Buzz," Britton put in. "Fleming threw his arm up in front of it. A thousand-to-one shot."

Pete gave the third baseman a glance of gratitude. But he was charged with an error on the throw and Smith was in a deep hole, no matter whose fault it might have been.

The reliever was equal to the occasion. He got the next hitter on a pop foul and then forced Joe Troyer to hit sharply to Britton for the "round the Horn" double play — third to second to first. Smith got a resounding cheer from the fans, and Pete, jogging behind him, would have wagged his tail had he been a dog. His throw had not cost anything.

"Now playing center field for the Hornets, Clampett," the public address system informed the crowd. High above the field, Ken Kirkpatrick said peevishly, "That's the second time Conroy has put Dixie out of action. Last time it cost us the game, too."

"You think he did it deliberately, Ken?" Floyd McGreevy asked incredulously. "He would have thrown at his head."

"Well, he did say he was going to drill Dixie, didn't he?" Kirkpatrick replied. McGreevy snorted.

As Wakely stepped up to face Jones in the last of the eleventh, Pete checked the batting order and saw that he would bat fourth. Wakely hit the first pitch down the left-field line for a double, and the crowd screamed in anticipation. Johnny Key dragged a good bunt down the line and Jones had to make the play at first, Wakely perching at third.

Freddie Villa went to the plate and Pete moved into the on deck circle, nerves starting to jump. Villa was a .240 hitter, but Kearns signaled Jones from the bench to walk him intentionally. He knew the Eagles could not pinch hit for Pete, for they were out of infielders if they failed to score. And with a man on first, the double play chances were enhanced.

Pete's pulse beat more rapidly as he saw the pitcher throwing wide to Villa. Meredith called him back to the bench as Freddie tossed away his bat and went to first.

"Don't try to kill the ball, just meet it," the manager advised. "I don't think he'll try to deck you now. He won't risk it."

Nevertheless, Pete, holding his bat high, kept one foot slightly to the rear, ready to duck away if needed. But all Jones wanted was an out and the first ball was down the middle for a strike. The second was high inside for a ball, and next a slider for another called strike.

Pete tightened his grip on the bat. He was not going down just looking, he thought grimly. Jones came over the top with another slider. Pete lashed at it and raised a fly to straightaway center.

The Hornet outfield was playing shallow, since a long fly would score the runner anyway and would be as good as a hit. Clampett had to move back only a few feet. Pete fled toward first, reaching it as the ball dropped into the Hornet's glove.

Wakely was waiting for the catch and he took off. He would have been sent in even if Fleming, with an outstanding arm, had been in center, since the pitcher was due to bat next.

Possibly Fleming would have thrown Wakely out at the plate. Clampett did not. His peg was a few feet up the line toward third, the catcher had to move up to get it, and the runner was past him before he could dive futilely in the effort to make the tag.

The stands erupted joyfully and Ken Kirkpatrick, slamming his score book shut, said bitterly, "One way to win a ball game — knock out the other team's big man."

CHAPTER 14

"IT's A GOOD THING you don't play the Hornets on this trip, Buzz," Floyd McGreevy said. "I don't think the place would be safe, especially for Conroy."

Meredith said irritably, "Why don't you writers get off this feud kick for a while? We're in the middle of a red-hot pennant race and you keep harping on some minor beef between two players."

"One of 'em happens to be the league's leading hitter," McGreevy pointed out, "and he's out of action for three, four days. He was out once before, remember, and Conroy figured in that one, too. Call it coincidence if you want, but don't think that's what the Hornets call it."

The two men were in the airline terminal waiting for the plane that was to take the team on another road trip, 15 games in 13 days. Three doubleheaders were on the schedule, to make up games canceled by rain earlier in the year. Although the swing included the weaker teams, the Rams, Capitols, and Robins, Meredith was far from over-confident. It was now mid-August, and the heat was excessive. Pitchers like Gregg and

Shipstein had trouble going nine innings under those conditions. The bullpen was in for lots of work on this trip.

"When do you play the Hornets again?" McGreevy asked.

"We finish the season with them."

"Here or there?"

"There," Meredith said moodily. "Maybe by that time we'll have the flag sewed up and nobody will care."

"I'm for that," the writer said heartily.

So was Pete Conroy, waiting in a group with Elwood, Berry, and Shipstein. He had scanned the schedule and was aware that his path would not cross Fleming's again for another six weeks. The furor over the final game with the Hornets two days before had made him uncomfortable, for he was also aware the visitors had left town with dire mutterings about "next time."

So he responded with irritation to Berry's casual remark.

"You know, Petey, if you keep knockin' that Dixie man out of the lineup, mebbe we'll win that little ol' pennant. Ah don't fear those Bengals or Chicks like Ah do the Hornets."

"Get off me, will you, Stu?" Pete snapped. Berry looked a bit wounded, and Elwood moved in hastily.

"Say, Pete, what do you hear from your old club, the Wildcats, out in the open spaces?"

"I haven't checked 'em for a couple of weeks,

Ace. Last time I looked, they were right where I left 'em — in fourth place."

"I guess you didn't hold 'em back too much," Shipstein said with heavy humor, and then it was time to board the plane.

The Rams, mired in seventh place, were the first stop for the Eagles. Shipstein went along steadily for seven innings, before he made what turned out to be a mistake. He hit a long drive over the right fielder's head and forced his heavy-legged frame around the bases for a triple.

That took more out of him than the seven innings of pitching. He gave up a walk and two singles before Meredith halted the proceedings and went out to talk to him.

"Guess I'm out of gas, Buzz," the pitcher said wryly. Meredith understood that. The Eagles' bullpen had been lightly active since the fifth inning despite a big lead, so he decided to call in Conroy. With an 8–2 working margin, he had room to experiment. The manager was curious to learn whether the latest Fleming incident had left any marks on Pete.

One run was in, and there were men on first and third when Pete, perspiring lightly from merely warming up, came on.

"Goodwin is strictly a fast-ball hitter," Meredith said, inclining his head toward the batter. "Slow up on him."

Tad Yerkes was the catcher. Pete wasted the fast ball outside, then threw the fork ball. Goodwin swung in front of it and popped to the infield.

"That's one, Pete," Freddie Villa said confidently, as he came over to the mound to hand Pete the ball. The next man got a good piece of an inside fast ball and raised a long fly to right. The runner scored after the catch, but Pete got the last man to swing on a sinking fast ball and walked off the hill with just the hint of a swagger.

That feeling vanished in the ninth, however, as he walked one man and gave up a double for the Rams' fourth run. Both De Anza and Berry were throwing hard when the game-ending out was produced on a grounder to Britton at shortstop.

Not good, not bad, Pete told himself. Still, he felt he had come a long way from Winston. Jim Varnell and Ace Elwood had taught him something; he was something more now than just a hard thrower.

Mike North beat the Rams next day, and Gregg, with help from Dolin and De Anza, made it three straight. But Bill Kosecki, Berry, and De Anza again were pasted hard in the first game of a doubleheader and in desperation Meredith selected Duane Smith to pitch the second game.

He did not last beyond the fourth in the seesaw battle that saw the lead change hands three times. Dolin came to his aid in that inning and pitched fairly well with the aid of some sensational fielding behind him. Pete Conroy had warmed up since the seventh. The field was not visible from the bullpen, but the crowd noises in the last of the ninth told Pete that the home team had something going. He got the call from the bench a moment later.

As he cut across the outfield, he looked up at the scoreboard, saw that the Eagles led, 7–6, and that two were out. He saw also that there were men on first and second. Dolin, looking depressed, handed him the ball without a word. Pete glanced past Elwood toward the plate, saw that the batter was Goodwin again.

"You know how to pitch to this guy," Meredith said, tension obvious in his manner. The prospect of losing a double-header to a second division team was not a happy one. "Show him the fast ball, then pull the string."

Elwood said, "Never mind the runners, Pete. Get this one and we can go home."

Pete was mildly surprised at his own lack of nervousness, despite the pressure of the situation. He was bolstered by the manager's confidence in him to get rid of Goodwin, and he meant to justify that confidence.

He leaned in for Elwood's sign and buzzed the fast ball shoulder high on the inside, to remind the batter that he had it. Elwood signaled for the letup pitch. Pete stretched, looked once at second base, kicked, and threw.

It was the fork ball, breaking down off the outside corner. Goodwin waited, swung and slammed it off the boards in left center as the runners raced around the bases. The second and winning run crossed the plate as Pete was turning in the useless attempt to make the relay for Phil Slade.

191

Pete Conroy stood on the mound, his thin features a study in despair. He should have gone to the plate to back up the catcher in the event the throw-in got past Elwood. But as he followed the ball's flight, he knew such a move would be needless.

Head down and shoulders drooping, he walked toward the dugout. Meredith said tonelessly, "Too bad, Pete. He got lucky." He did not sound convincing.

Pete sought out Elwood on the plane. "What was wrong with the one Goodwin hit, Ace?" he asked. "I thought it was right where it should have been."

"It was," the catcher replied. "But he guessed right. Don't feel too bad about it, Pete. Next time you'll get him with it."

The road trip proved something of a nightmare to Pete, and the number of batters he got out were discouragingly few. The Eagles won three out of four from the Robins to lead by two full games, and there was a stirring of World Series talk, studiously avoided heretofore.

None of that exciting prospect communicated itself to Pete. In the one game the Eagles dropped to the Robins, he relieved in the eighth with one man on and one out, trailing 7–2. He yielded a double at once on what he thought was a good fast ball before retiring the side. Stu Berry pitched the ninth.

Nor was he effective against the light-hitting Capitols. He pitched the eighth inning against them in a game the Eagles had already lost, for all practical purposes. True, an error by the usually reliable Alten started him off poorly, but it was not Alten's fault that it was followed by a single and then a long fly that disappeared into the right-field bleachers for a home run.

He retired the next two men, walked the third, and finally finished the inning on a hard smash hit right at Villa. He had the sinking feeling that he might not be called upon again soon.

In that he was quite correct. The Eagles split four games with the Gold Sox, and only one starter, Bill Kosecki, went the distance. In the other three games, the bullpen was almost constantly active, Pete excepted. Each time the phone rang, he eyed Varnell hopefully, but the coach always pointed to another. Considering the way he had been manhandled in his last three appearances, Pete could not blame Meredith for his lack of faith.

The chilling aspect of that was Pete's inability to fathom what had suddenly gone wrong with his pitching. He had not been unusually wild; he had been throwing as hard as before and his change-up had improved, he firmly believed, under Varnell's tutelage. Nor had he served up any of the flat curves that a batter could follow easily. No, they were hitting his best pitches.

Maybe I'm not a pitcher, after all, he thought sadly. Perhaps he had only been lucky at first and now that batters had had the opportunity to study him, they were able to handle him the second time around. Yet he could not bring himself to believe that was the entire answer.

Much the same questions were raised in a conference among Meredith, Varnell, and Ace Elwood the day after the Eagles returned home. It was an open date, and a highly welcome one, for the Bengals, Chicks, and Generals were coming in for the September drive toward the flag, still contenders all.

"Why are they teeing off on Conroy recently?" Meredith demanded querulously. "He can't seem to get a strike past anyone."

"Beats me," the catcher said helplessly. "It looks like the same stuff he was throwing a month ago and they couldn't find him most of the time then."

"Any chance they're stealing signs on us?" Varnell asked speculatively.

Meredith scowled. "If so, why aren't they stealing 'em on our other pitchers? Could be that Conroy's doing something to tip off his pitch, though. Something that tells 'em whether it's going to be the fast ball or the change. Does he show 'em the ball before he stretches, Jim? He holds it differently for the fork ball; the first-base coach could spot that."

"No," Varnell said emphatically. "I checked him on that first time he pitched. He doesn't fix his grip until he's ready to throw. It has to be something else, if that's the reason they're banging him. And it's not his motion, either, because he throws everything the same way. Right, Ace?"

Elwood agreed.

Pete was in low spirits as he sat in the locker room the night of the opener of the Bengal series. A familiar figure walked in, paused, and surveyed the room, then came directly toward Pete.

"Hello, laddie." Foxy Thurlow said with a grin and an extended hand. "How goes it?"

"Not too good, Foxy," Pete said gloomily. "My arm feels fine and I think I know more about the business than I did when I came up. But they bomb me."

Thurlow was sympathetic. "I noticed you haven't been as effective as you were earlier. Tell me, Pete, does the Fleming thing bother you? I've read a lot about that."

"Sure it bothered me," Pete conceded. "But it had nothing to do with what happened to me on this last road trip. How could it?"

"I don't know; maybe it was weighing on your mind. I'd forget it if I could."

"I'm trying," Pete said dourly.

"Well, I'll see you later. I have to tell Buzz what's happening out in the wilderness. Thank goodness I can sleep in the same bed two nights running for a while."

Meredith, feet cocked on his desk, greeted Thurlow warmly. They talked for a while about Eagle farmhands who might be recalled later in the month, when the minor league season ended.

"There're only a couple who look like they could help us even a little, and none of them are pitchers," the manager groused. "If they were, I would've had 'em up here long ago."

"I think Wykoff might come in handy, Buzz. He's a flashy fielder even if he doesn't hit."

"Shortstops who can't hit I've got plenty of now. Anyway, I can use Conroy in a pinch; I have already a couple of times."

"Oh, yes, Conroy," Thurlow said casually. "How's he doing?"

Meredith concealed his amusement. He was quite aware that the scout was eager to talk about his own discovery.

"Frankly, Foxy, he's got me puzzled. He started off well, but lately he's been getting nothing but lumps. They've been nailing him the second time they've seen him and that's a surprise, because he hasn't been used much. We've been thinking he might be tipping off his pitches, but we don't know how."

Thurlow made a steeple of his fingers. "You plan to use him on this home stand?"

"Right now he's a body in the bullpen. I'll use him if I have to, because we're on the short line for relievers. But it will be in spots where he can't hurt us."

"O.K., Buzz. Good luck, and I may see you afterward."

The Eagles needed more than luck that night; they needed runs. A big right-hander named Crevelow shut them out with four hits, the defense made three costly errors, and Mike North was behind, 6–0, after eight innings.

It was a situation to which Meredith had referred, where a reliever could hardly do the cause any appreciable damage. As Pete Conroy emerged from the bullpen, Foxy Thurlow, who had been watching the game from a seat behind third base, moved to another vacant seat almost directly back of the plate.

Pete's face was a study in determination as he warmed up with Charlie Temple. But it hid the uncertainty in his mind. He no longer had full confidence in his pitches.

A little of it began to seep back as he disposed of the first batter on four straight fast balls, the cross fire getting him swinging and missing by six inches.

"He ought to get them out with that one," Thurlow muttered.

The next man hit a bad hop grounder that hit the surprised Jim Grey in the shoulder for a cheap hit. Pete remained undismayed, but not for long. The next hitter singled off the fork ball and his successor slashed a double to left. Sweating profusely, Pete got the next Bengal on a pop to the infield.

But a bat-handle blooper into right drove both men home, the runner going to second on the throw to the plate. By this time, Pete was plunged in misery and completely bewildered. He knew he had as much stuff as he ever had, yet he was being shelled as though he were merely lobbing the ball to the plate.

He expected Meredith to come out and get him, but the manager remained at his usual place on the dugout steps, wincing inwardly as the hits continued. He could not understand the Bengals' success, either. His pitcher appeared to be throwing hard and accurately.

Desperate, Pete threw his next pitch out of Temple's reach, and the runner streaked to third. But he finished the inning as the batter watched the letup clip the corner of the plate for a called third strike.

Foxy Thurlow got up and began to move through the crowd, already beginning to depart, toward the Eagles' club house. He was sitting in Meredith's office when the manager came in, tossing his cap against the wall and plopping wearily into his chair.

"Grim, wasn't it?" he said. "You saw what I meant about Conroy?"

"I saw that he was telegraphing every pitch with men on bases," Thurlow said mildly. "I was calling them myself toward the end of the inning. He had good stuff, Buzz, but if I could tell what was coming, I'm sure they could do it, too. No wonder the kid's been getting blasted."

Meredith sat up as though jabbed with a pin, his pale blue eyes boring into Thurlow's face.

"You're sure?" he asked skeptically.

Foxy shrugged. "Reasonably sure. Did you notice that he got strikeouts and a pop-up when he was pitching from the full windup instead of from the stretch?"

Meredith reviewed the inning in his mind. "That's right, he did," he acknowledged with heightened interest. "O.K., tell me how he gives it away."

Thurlow told him, with extensive motions.

"Well, I'll be — " Meredith exclaimed in amazement. "That simple, and we couldn't see it when everyone else could. It's hard to believe, Foxy."

"Not so hard," the scout said. "I happened to be looking for it. Art Mahaffey of the Phillies did the same thing all through one season, nobody on his club saw it, and he won 19 games anyway. It wasn't until one of the players who knew it was traded to the Phils that Art learned what it was. The batters knew whether to expect the fast ball or the curve, but he got 'em out anyway. He happens to be a better pitcher than Pete Conroy."

Meredith said thoughtfully, "I remember that about Mahaffey. Did you notice Conroy doing it when you watched him in the minors?"

"They weren't hitting him there," Foxy said dryly. "That's why I recommended him."

Meredith had to grin. "I'd like to check this myself. I'll have Conroy out at eleven tomorrow. Want to watch?"

"What do you think?" Thurlow asked.

Pete Conroy, his spirits lower than they had been a dozen hours earlier and even more confused, walked out into the sunlight with Ace Elwood.

"Honestly, I don't know, Pete," the catcher said.

"Buzz said he wanted me suited up by 11. Isn't that what he told you?"

"Yes, but he didn't say why," Pete said plaintively. "Evidently I'm going to do some throwing to you, but what for, after last night?"

"Come on, Pete. Charlie said you were humming it."

"What if I did? You saw what they did to it."

Before Elwood could answer, Meredith and Foxy Thurlow came out of the dugout, increasing Pete's mystification.

"Get loosened up, Pete," the manager directed crisply. "I want you ready to bear down in a few minutes."

He ordered the grounds keepers to wheel the batting cage into position at the plate. After five minutes, Pete announced that his arm was sufficiently loosened up to pitch. Meredith got a bat and Elwood, aghast, asked, "Do I need the mask, Buzz?"

"No, I'm only going to give Conroy a target. Ace, I want you to call for each pitch as though you were in a game. Pete, there's a man on first. Work from the stretch."

He stepped to the plate. Thurlow stationed himself behind the cage, just off Elwood's right shoulder.

Pete could only guess at the nature of the test he was being given. He got the catcher's sign, stretched, and pitched.

As his arm flashed down, Meredith said loudly, "Fast ball."

200

Fast ball it was, and the crouching Elwood looked up at him in surprise. The manager had not turned his head.

"Fast ball," he called again as Pete uncoiled. He was right.

Fork ball, fast ball, change-up — Meredith called off the next half dozen deliveries unerringly before the ball had left Pete's hand. Pete understood by then what the test was disclosing. He was, in some manner, letting the batter know what was coming. Frantically he went over the details of his delivery, seeking to find the flaw. Ball hidden? Yes. Arm motion? Leg kick? Not that he was aware of; they were the same, he was sure, for all pitches.

Meredith held up a hand and beckoned to him. Pete walked toward him like an errant child about to be punished for some wrongdoing he did not understand. Elwood straightened and gazed in bafflement as Foxy Thurlow sauntered around the cage to join the group.

"I suppose you've guessed what this is all about," Buzz said. "Pete, you've been tipping off your pitch and the hitters have been laying back knowing whether they'll get the hummer or the change. Even if they don't know whether it's coming in high or low, inside or outside, it gives them quite an edge. Foxy saw it right away last night. Tell him, Foxy."

Thurlow said tolerantly, "Pete, go back to the mound and take the stretch. You're going to throw the fork ball."

Pete obeyed, looking over his shoulder at the imaginary runner on first, then raising his arms, and bringing them down.

"All right, look at your hands."

Pete glanced down. His gloved hand covered the other, both resting against his belt.

"Now," Foxy directed, "you're throwing the fast ball."

Pete repeated the motion.

"Look at your hands again."

Pete looked down, saw nothing different. He felt stupid, as though his hands were talking and he could not hear them.

"You see?" Foxy asked. Pete shook his head mutely.

"By gravy, I think I do!" Elwood exclaimed in some excitement. "Hold that position, Pete."

He turned to Thurlow. "When he comes down for the letup, he's right at his belt. For the fast ball, he holds it lower and a little away from his body. Is that it?"

Meredith said, "Right." Thurlow smiled deprecatingly.

Pete stared down again at his telltale hands. Sure enough, they were slightly below his belt and perhaps an inch from his body. Enough difference for a sharp-eyed observer to pick it up and turn against him.

He dropped his arms and walked toward the group, his mind whirling. "I must have been doing that unconsciously all the time," he said in a small voice.

"It's happened to others," Meredith said gruffly. "Maybe this isn't the whole answer to why you've been hammered lately, but it could be. It doesn't take long for it to get around."

"Thanks, Foxy," Pete said, bewildered and shaken. Thurlow glanced at Meredith.

"Think nothing of it, Pete. I was protecting my investment."

Meredith had the grace to laugh.

CHAPTER 15

BARNEY FLAIG, the bowlegged, gravel-voiced manager of the Chicks, stood outside the dugout chatting with Buzz Meredith in the midday sunlight. The two were rivals but also old friends. They talked aimlessly about umpires and ballplayers and games won and lost, exchanging mutual complaints but no secrets.

It was Flaig who brought up the subject of Dixie Fleming. "You finish on the road, don't you?"

"Yep, the last week. Three with the Generals, two with the Hornets. I wish it were the other way around, frankly."

"Somebody has to be the visiting team," Flaig rumbled. "You're probably in for a hot time when you hit the Hornets."

"I suppose so." Meredith's face clouded. "You mean Fleming?"

Flaig nodded. "We played 'em last week," he said, frowning at the recollection. "The writers, anyway, were still complaining about your guy putting Dixie out of action twice. He missed six games and they lost five of them. They can show you on paper at least, how they would have won 'em with Dixie in there, and that would have put 'em on top now. We split four games with 'em, and I gotta admit Fleming hurt us plenty."

"I'm sick of those choke artists riding Conroy!" Buzz said angrily. "He and Dixie don't like each other, but my man is the one who ought to complain. It's not Fleming's fault he isn't on the disabled list right now, I'll tell you that."

"So I hear," Flaig said, unruffled. "But I thought you'd like to know. Anyway, maybe you two will be fighting for fourth place by that time. I hope so."

"The same to you and many of them," Buzz retorted, grinning.

Pete Conroy sat with the bullpen crew that afternoon, as fidgety as a schoolgirl at a dance. He wanted to put Foxy Thurlow's theory to the test, but in the final two games with the Bengals, both taken by the Eagles, there had been only one call for a reliever and that had brought Sil De Anza to the mound.

During those two days, Pete had gone over in his memory the bad pitches he had made. He had no trouble recalling them, beginning with Dixie Fleming's game-winning triple. Sure enough, there was a discernible pattern. Nearly every time that one of his good deliveries had been nailed, Pete had been pitching from the stretch position.

It was still only a theory, he reminded himself. It might also be a string of unfortunate coincidences stemming from the fact that he was still not a pitcher.

His chance came in the eighth inning that day as Bill Kosecki, pitching carefully, led the Chicks, 4–1. A single by the Chicks leadoff was the signal for the Eagles' bullpen to go to work. Pete's pulses quickened as Varnell pointed to him and Duane Smith.

Kosecki, weakening slightly, gave up a walk and another single after two outs, and the score was 4–2 when Meredith decided to make a change.

"O.K., Pete, go get 'em," Stu Berry called. Pete went through the gate with the feeling that this might be one of the most important innings of his career.

A left-handed pinch hitter named Browning was waiting to face him. All Meredith said was, "Keep it low."

There were runners at first and third and Pete warmed up from the stretch position, careful to bring his hands down to his belt in the same way each time. If the hitters were going to guess him, they would do so hereafter without outside help.

Browning took a low fast ball inside at the knees for a called strike and laid off another that was too low. Pete came in with the change-up and Browning started to swing, checked, and fell away. The ball hit his bat and bounced lazily to Jim Grey at third, who gunned it to first for the final out.

Ace Elwood joined Pete on the way in. "He wasn't expecting that one," he said significantly. "He was looking for the fast ball."

"It was a fluke."

"Flukes count."

The Eagles picked up a run in their half of the eighth. Pete went out to pitch the ninth, but did not complete it. He got rid of the first batter on an infield grounder, but then walked one. Elwood came out to tell him to take his time and Pete got the next man on a cross fire that was lofted to right.

But the following hitter slammed a high fast ball to center for a double, scoring a run, and Meredith took no chances. As he waited at the mound for Duane Smith to arrive, the manager said, "What was that last one?"

"I got it up too high," Pete said, crestfallen.

"I'll say this, Buzz," Elwood put in. "I don't think they were reading him."

Meredith merely grunted. But after Smith had induced the Chicks' hitter to pop up and end the game, the manager was rather pleased about Pete. The big out of the game, as he saw it, was the one Pete had gotten to end the Chicks' threat in the eighth, the rally-snuffer. A pitcher who gets the one out necessary in the clutch was invaluable, even if he did not face another batter after that. Particularly in September.

There had rarely been a pennant race like it, the baseball writers kept pointing out to their readers. Two-team races, even three-team races right down to the wire were not infrequent. But not in the memory of any baseball historian had the season entered its final week with five teams still having a chance.

Yet that was how it stood with just six playing dates remaining — the Eagles leading by a single game, the Hornets and the Generals tied for second, the Chicks a game behind them, and the Bengals fifth, only three games out.

In the rival league, the Tigers had already won the race and marked time, waiting for their World Series opponent to be determined.

The Eagles had doggedly withstood challenges all through the month. Pennant fever was raging in their clubhouse and Pete had been infected with it like everyone else. Until this frenzied stretch drive, he had been too deeply immersed in his own personal problems to think even vaguely of a World Series.

But as the end drew nearer, the realization that every game won was a step closer to the championship, every error, every bad pitch might prove the difference between first place and second, even fifth, began to have its effects.

Clubhouse celebrations after a victory were noisier than before; gloom and snappish tempers intensified after a loss. "We'll get 'em tomorrow," was a comment frequently heard after a defeat, but not in September. The players knew they were running out of tomorrows.

Pete pitched on two more occasions during the home stand. He came in to face the Generals with men on first and third and one out in the sixth, kept his fast ball low, and forced the batter to hit to Freddie Villa for the double play.

That was all that Meredith required of him in that game.

"I don't know for sure if a lot of hitters were reading Conroy before," Elwood told Meredith, "but I don't think it would have made any difference on that pitch. When his control is right, he's awful tough."

"I think he's got his confidence back," the manager said. "For a while he was throwing as if everything he served up would go out of the park. I must buy Foxy a dinner sometime."

The manager was correct; Pete had regained his confidence to a considerable degree. He was going to be hit, he knew, because the ball did not always go where he wanted it to go. But he felt that if he could get his cross fire or fork ball around the corners and keep them low, the chances of the batter hitting it anywhere but on the ground were reduced.

His effort against the Rams was not crowned with success. Yet miserable as Pete felt about it, he was even sorrier for Wykoff, the rookie infielder up from New Bristol.

Freddie Villa came down with a heavy cold the day of the game, and Don Snyder took his place in the lineup at second base. Snyder was lifted to let Charlie Temple bat for him in the bottom of the eighth when the Eagles tied the score, to the delight of the large midweek crowd.

Wykoff went out to play second base in the ninth.

The first two men to face De Anza singled and once again, Pete came to work.

The batter was Goodwin, who had ruined Pete's day the last time they had faced each other. Pete struck him out on five pitches, jamming him inside for the final swinging strike, and Goodwin bounced his bat disgustedly in front of the dugout.

The next man hit the ball a solid smash, but on one hop to Leo Brown at shortstop, Brown fired to Wykoff, who first dropped the ball and then, in a frantic effort to recover, picked it up and threw it three feet out of Dave Alten's reach at first. The runner on third scored and when the ball had finally been retrieved, there were Rams on second and third, and still only one out.

Wykoff, futilely banging his fist into his glove, looked as though he was about to cry. Pete, shocked and momentarily outraged at the compound error, nevertheless felt his sympathy go out to the unhappy rookie. He recalled feeling the same way toward Halligan under similar circumstances years ago when he was manager of the Winston Wildcats. Years ago? It had been only a few months.

Meredith signaled to Elwood to have Pete walk the next man intentionally to fill the bases. Pete was not surprised when Stu Berry was called in to pitch to the left-handed batter who followed. Berry got him out, but on a long fly that scored the runner from third and the Eagles lost it, 6–4.

From that day until the very last day of the season, Wykoff was used only as a pinch runner.

Meredith did not want that error to prey on the rookie's mind in the stretch drive. When the time came, however, he had no choice.

Richie Shipstein said, in a little-boy tone, "You know, I've never been in a World Series. I wonder if I ever will."

"Come on, Richie," Alten chided. "All we have to do is win the next five and we're in."

"The next five. You make it sound easy."

"It's the easiest way. Can't depend on the others to help."

The Eagles were riding out from the hotel in the team bus for the first of their three games with the Generals. Pete, sitting behind the pair, knew how Shipstein must feel. He was pitching that night against the Generals. North would pitch the second game, Gregg, the third and then, after the day between series, Shipstein would be up again for the opener against the Hornets.

Pete sympathized with Richie, but he himself did not feel that sort of pressure. He did not think his number would go up with so much at stake and so many veterans available.

There were five teams in the race on Tuesday. By Thursday night, the list had been reduced to two, the Eagles and the Hornets. The Eagles took two out of three from the Generals, who were thus eliminated; the Hornets kept pace with two out of three from the Bengals, who also dropped out of contention, and the Gold Sox ruined the Chicks' last chance by taking one.

"Well," said Buzz Meredith to Varnell, as they boarded the plane that night, "here we go."

The Eagles needed one win out of the two games; the Hornets had to win both.

"SHOWDOWN FOR THE PENNANT!" That's the way the headlines read when the Eagles arrived. A "Welcome Eagles" banner hung across the marquee of their hotel, but somehow it seemed to lack sincerity.

To keep the players from becoming too restless through idleness, Meredith ordered a light workout at the Hornets' stadium in the afternoon. The stands were empty, of course, but the field was aswarm with writers and cameramen.

"I see you brought your boy Conroy along," Ken Kirkpatrick remarked to Meredith, nodding to Pete, limbering up with Berry.

Meredith bristled, but was careful to reply in moderate tone. "Why not? He's on the roster. Anyone object?"

"No," the writer said hastily. "But you know what I'm talking about, Buzz. There's been trouble before."

Meredith pretended to be puzzled. "Has Fleming been making threats? I'll have to talk to Kearns about that."

Kirkpatrick flushed, aware that he was being needled. "Nobody's made any threats," he said sourly. "The only one I know about is the one Conroy made to drill Dixie the next time. Right after that, he hit him on the elbow and benched

212

him. Sure, it was an accident, but the fact remains Conroy did say it."

"Well, he's pitched since then and hasn't hit anyone," Meredith growled. "Why don't we play the ball game? This isn't a war, you know."

Secretly, he was a little disturbed, but firmly determined to resist intimidation. Pete Conroy did not figure in his plans for this series, but if Meredith felt he could be useful, no implied threats were going to stop him.

Yet the Hornet fans seemed to be almost warlike in their reception next day. Pete was jarred at the roar of boos that followed the announcement of each name in the Eagles' lineup. The blanket indictment from the packed stadium was more than he had expected.

"Nice bunch," Dave Alten said sarcastically as the raucous sounds cascaded across the field.

"The gun's pointed at their heads," Phil Slade said. "If they don't win today, they're dead. We have another chance."

"I'd as soon have a day off tomorrow," Alten retorted.

Except for Dan Dolin, who had a stiffness in his shoulder, and Mike North, who was to pitch the last game, the Eagles' relief crew that set out on the long walk to the bullpen before the game included every pitcher on the staff. Gregg and Kosecki, the regular starters, were among them. Meredith felt the need to spare nobody if the Eagles could win today. If that happened, the bat boy could pitch for them the next day for all it mattered.

The relievers had to walk close to the stands and they were heckled all the way. A crumpled paper beverage cup sailed from the stands and landed at the feet of Stu Berry. He kicked it aside angrily and Jim Varnell said sharply, "Don't blow up, Stu." Muttering, Berry stomped on.

Grady Jones was opposing Shipstein on the mound and the fans cheered madly as Jim Grey struck out to open the game. That set the pattern for the day. Every ball called against Jones was disputed from the stands, every strike met with applause. The reverse was true when the Hornets batted.

Shipstein pitched to only five men. Tex White, second man to face him in the second inning, smashed a low line drive right back at the box. Richie had just enough time to get his glove down. The ball ricocheted off it, struck him on the shin, and dropped him as though he had been slugged on the jaw.

White was safe, of course, but Shipstein, in considerable pain, had to be helped from the field. Had he not deflected the ball with his glove, his leg might have been broken.

Meredith, his forehead creased with concern, waved in Jack Gregg, who was given all the time he thought necessary, since he was replacing an injured man. The fans began to growl impatiently as Jack continued to throw leisurely, but he was

214

too old a campaigner to be ruffled by crowd noises.

The Hornets scored two in the third, setting off bedlam in the stadium. It was not all Gregg's fault, for one of three hits in that inning was a pop-up back of second that Leo Brown got his glove on but could not hold.

In the top of the fourth, the Eagles put two men on base with two out, and Meredith did not hesitate to lift Gregg to let Charlie Temple bat for him unsuccessfully. The Eagles could not win without runs even if Jack blanked the Hornets the rest of the way.

Kosecki came on to pitch the fourth, walked the first two men, and was pulled out immediately. De Anza replaced him, but the Hornets picked up another run before he could get the side out.

Jones got into more difficulty in the sixth. With one out, Elwood singled, and Freddie Villa lined a screamer to left for two bases, Ace holding at third. Meredith sent Tad Yerkes up to swing for the light-hitting Leo Brown, aware that Yerkes would probably be walked intentionally to force the Eagles to use another pinch hitter for the pitcher. This he was quite willing to do; the Eagles had to take their scoring opportunities when they arose. They could not wait until later.

Yerkes was walked, on orders, and the fleet Don Snyder was put in to run for him. Jarvis stalked to the plate to bat for De Anza. In the bullpen, Duane Smith began to fire harder.

Jarvis gave it a good try. He slammed a grounder that handcuffed the second baseman momentarily, but the Hornet had time to pick it up and throw Jarvis out at first. The run scored but Jim Grey ended the rally by flying deep to Fleming.

As Smith picked up his jacket and departed to pitch the sixth, Varnell ordered Stu Berry and Pete to start throwing. They were all that were left of the men that had entered.

Dave Alten hit a towering bases-empty home run in the eighth to make it 3–2, Smith held the Hornets at bay, and the Eagles came out for the ninth needing a run.

Jones slipped a strike past Villa, and the crowd yelled, but Freddie then hung a clothesline single over second, and the fans stirred nervously.

Meredith's throat was dry and cottony. He had to have Bobby Britton bunt Villa along, of course, but he was in trouble for pinch hitters if he elected to have someone swing for Smith. He had only Wykoff and another youngster from New Bristol, an outfielder named Hart, left on his bench. They were slender reeds in this emergency.

Britton bunted, in front of the plate. The Hornet catcher pounced on it and rifled it down to second — into the dirt. It came up bouncing off the shortstop's chest and all hands were safe as the fans groaned.

By this time, bullpen activity had stopped, and Pete, with the others, had his nose pressed against the fence. Meredith gulped in gratitude for the catcher's error. Smith was not a bad bunter; he could bat for himself. He sent the speedy Hart out to run for Britton.

Smith bunted. Even though the pitcher and first baseman were charging the ball, Smith got it down the line toward third, and Jones had to go to first with the throw.

Jim Grey was walked intentionally to load the bases for the double-play possibility, but Johnny Key made hash of that Hornet strategy, sound though it was, with a grass cutter between first and second. Villa and Hart stormed home as the Eagles' bench erupted in a war dance and a pall of gloom settled over the stands.

In the midst of the uproar, Meredith remembered that he was going to need a shortstop. Wykoff was still on the bench, but Buzz did not want the untried youngster out there in a situation like this. He had another man, slower, but one who had been through the mill. He grabbed the bullpen phone.

"Get going, shortstop," Jim Varnell said. Pete, who had gone into a wild embrace with Berry as Hart scored the leading run, disentangled himself and stared at Varnell. Then he pushed open the gate and ran, forgetting his warm-up jacket.

The Eagles' bench was still boiling joyously and nobody paid him any attention until the inning was over. By that time, they had scored again off Jones's reliever, Tippett, as Phil Slade singled Key to third, and Alten sent him in after a sacrifice fly.

So it was 5–3 as Pete went out to play shortstop. There was a despairing note in the fans' pleas for the Hornets to start something. Even the jeers which greeted the announcement that Conroy was now playing shortstop seemed halfhearted, Pete smiled to himself.

Boo your ears off, you donkeys, he thought. You're licked and you know it.

But they weren't quite beaten yet. Smith lost the first batter on a ball-four call that was very close. He stamped angrily around the mound, kicking at the dirt, as Elwood came out to calm him. Meredith ordered Mike North to the bullpen to loosen up, as a final precaution.

Another pinch hitter faced Smith, hit one to Grey, who had to make the toss to first as Smith covered.

"One," Pete counted silently, certain that every other Eagle was making the same countdown. Chuck Mackey grounded to Villa, who threw him out as the runner moved to third.

"Two," Pete breathed. Joe Troyer stepped to the plate, and Smith's first pitch hit him on the arm. The sound from the crowd was now an unbroken roar as Buzz Meredith came slowly to the center of the diamond. Smith, his face white and drawn, stared at the ball as though it were a snake.

"I had the first man struck out," he protested in a shaky voice. "It ought to be all over by rights."

"Yeah," Meredith said. He did not have to look to see who Smith would face next. It was Dixie Fleming.

"Come on, Meredith, let's get it moving," the

plate umpire said as he came up to the group around the mound.

"O.K., O.K.," he said irritably. Smith was obviously upset and he did not want to leave him in. But all he had left in the bullpen were the two southpaws, Berry and North, and Fleming's chances of pulling one into the left-field seats would be enhanced.

"Conroy," he said suddenly. "Your arm loose? You think you could keep the ball inside the park on this guy?"

Pete, standing on the fringe on the group, gaped at him, not grasping the full import of the question at first. When he did, there was only one possible answer.

"Sure, Buzz."

Meredith turned to the umpire and pointed at Pete. "He's pitching. Wykoff!"

The rookie grabbed his glove and scurried onto the field. Pete, a trifle dazed, mechanically accepted the ball from Smith and stepped to the rubber. The knot of players broke up, only Elwood remaining.

"You know what to do with this man, Pete," the catcher said.

Pete looked toward the plate. Dixie Fleming was nervously banging his bat on the ground and Pete knew that he, too, felt the weight of the world on his shoulders.

On the dugout steps, Buzz Meredith was rationalizing the move he had just made. If Fleming hit safely, Mike North could still come in to throw against the left-handed hitter, Gaines. After all, the Hornets needed three runs to win. But if Dixie did hit the homer, he, Buzz Meredith, would be second-guessed as the biggest numbskull in the major leagues.

Pete really did not hear the announcement that he was now pitching, nor the hoots that followed, as he warmed up. He had been throwing in the bullpen since the sixth inning and the five pitches allotted him were enough to get his arm limber again.

Fleming stepped to the plate, determination written in the set of his mouth. Gone from Pete's mind was any thought of personal bitterness against Dixie; he might have been faceless. This was simply a pitcher against a batter for all the marbles.

Fleming would be aiming at the fences. Elwood knew it and signaled for the fork ball, the letup pitch.

Pete toed the rubber and stretched. As he did, an idea came to him as though by electricity. If Fleming once thought he could read Pete's pitches, there was nothing to be lost in trying to mislead him. When he brought his hands down, he deliberately held them below his belt and away from his body, the way he had telegraphed his fast ball before.

Pete kicked and threw. He never knew whether Fleming thought he was tipping off his pitch, but Dixie was certainly looking for and hoping for the hummer. He was stepping into the ball as it neared the plate, ready to tie into it. But he realized he would be out in front of it if he did. He checked his swing and took a called strike.

Elwood called for time and practically ran to the mound. "Watch your hands, Pete," he warned. "You were tipping again."

"Was I? If so, he got a bum steer. Think it over."

Elwood's brow furrowed. Then he said, "For the love of Mike! All right, cross him up, but don't cross me."

Ace asked for the fast ball. Pete came down off the stretch to his belt. Fleming shifted his front foot a bit and set himself. Pete poured it in, knee high and breaking off the outside corner. Dixie swung at it, but late.

Straight up the ball climbed, higher and higher in front of the mound. Pete moved forward under it, exultation rising in him and paying no heed to Jim Grey's shouts that he had it.

"Mine," he yelled joyfully and waved both arms. This out was indeed his, regardless of who should make the catch under the custom of letting an infielder do it. The startled Grey veered off and Pete felt the ball plunk into his glove.

He clutched it to make sure for perhaps five seconds, then turned, and threw it blindly up again in the direction of right field, before he was all but knocked down by the rush of his teammates, grabbing and pounding at him.

Elwood put both arms around Pete's middle and lifted him off the ground in a mighty bear hug.

"The Series! We're in the Series!" he yelled.

"Lemme down! Lemme down!" Pete gasped. He had just thought of something. Elwood released him and he broke through the mob of Eagles toward the Hornet dugout. Willie Gaines, who would have been the next hitter, threw his bat at the rack.

"Willie, Willie Gaines," Pete shouted. "Take a message to Dixie for me, will you?"

Gaines looked at him with eyes empty of hope.

"Tell him," Pete gurgled happily, "Tell him that I forgive him."

Then he turned to protect himself anew against the rough embraces of his teammates.